D0095094

Pieces of Payne

Other Books by Albert Goldbarth

POETRY

Coprolites
Jan. 31
Opticks
Keeping
A Year of Happy
Comings Back
Different Fleshes
Who Gathered and Whispered Behind Me
Faith
Original Light: New & Selected Poems 1973–1983
Arts & Sciences
Popular Culture
Heaven and Earth: A Cosmology
The Gods
Across the Layers: Poems Old and New
Marriage, and Other Science Fiction
A Lineage of Ragpickers
Adventures in Ancient Egypt
Beyond
Troubled Lovers in History
Saving Lives

PROSE

A Sympathy of Souls
Great Topics of the World
Dark Waves and Light Matter
Many Circles: New and Selected Essays

Pieces of Payne

Albert Goldbarth

Graywolf Press
SAINT PAUL, MINNESOTA

Publication of this volume is made possible in part by a grant provided by the Minnesota State Arts Board, through an appropria-
tion by the Minnesota State Legislature; a grant from the Wells
Fargo Foundation Minnesota; and a grant from the National
Endowment for the Arts. Significant support has also been provided by the Bush Foundation; Marshall Field's Project Imagine
with support from the Target Foundation; the McKnight Foundation; and other generous contributions from foundations, corpo-
rations, and individuals. To these organizations and individuals
we offer our heartfelt thanks.

Published by Graywolf Press
2402 University Avenue, Suite 203
Saint Paul, Minnesota 55114
All rights reserved.

www.graywolfpress.org

Printed in Canada
Published in the United States of America

ISBN 1-55597-378-7

2 4 6 8 9 7 5 3 1
First Graywolf Printing, 2003

Library of Congress Control Number: 2002111751

Cover design: Kyle G. Hunter
Cover art:
François Clouet, *Diane de Poitiers* (details), c. 1571. © 2002 Corbis
Mammogram courtesy Corbis. © 2002 Corbis
Cover constellation:
Cancer, the faintest constellation in the night sky

for Skyler
100 percent

contents

[1] *Indications of footnotes occur throughout the section "Pieces of Payne," and the texts of these—some brief, some lengthy—are collected in the "Notes" section. Each may be turned to as its number is first encountered, and so read singly, as a kind of erratic punctuation to "Pieces of Payne"; or they may be read as one continuous block of prose called "Notes"; or they may be read through any mixture of these two approaches. In a sense, they are pieces of "Pieces of Payne," and their repiecing is at the reader's discretion.*

. . . the great Cancer cluster, a close packed, ball-like mass of hundreds of shining suns, gathered together there like a great hive of swarming stars.

—EDMOND HAMILTON, *Outside the Universe*

Pieces of Payne

Every three minutes: a positive diagnosis (in the United States, one woman in eight, at some point in her life). And every fourteen minutes: a death ("the rate has changed very little since the 1930s"—Barbara Ehrenreich, "Welcome to Cancerland"). This is the background. This, and the scintillant drizzle of stars across the night sky, and the whale, and the werewolf, and the snick of a key unlocking a door at a cheap motel along I-35.

And here is how it begins, since we need to declare *some* entryway: a story is being told to me: and in it, a willful child is venting a teakettle steamhead of peevishness.

～

"Whyyyyy?"

"When daddy gets home from work, he first needs to rest by himself for a while."

"But *whyyyyy?*" Not *any* whine: the whine of a petulant three-year-old, dragged out through miles of piping.

And *then* what to say that might explain, yet still conceal?

"Because his job is . . . every day, he has to tell somebody a very sad thing."

"But *whyyyyy?*"—my friend Eliza remembers squealing the question in just that annoyingly long-drawn way. She imitates it; people look. We're having a drink (well, seven, as it turns out) after work. She's said she wants to request my "advice" on "something," and all these stories seem to be required as a prefatory gesture, although

3

most of them—the gold ring, the appointment book—I've heard before, and so have you: by now, the various surfaces we model onto an armature of childhood-angst-and-marital-infidelity are ubiquitous enough so that . . . look into your own friends' faces, and you'll find these narrative traces waiting for drink number three to unleash them.

(There's an image that comes to mind: someone who's falling, through a face the size of a firemen's net or a circus trampoline—and then she falls through another, and then another . . . all of the possible permutations of human faceness, and all of their stories.)

⌣

Two people *never* get divorced.

It's always a minimum of four.

And I don't mean merely adulterous liaisons—that lubricious pile of legs like writhing Pick Up Sticks, which seems to power so many sagas of marriages disintegrating.

No, I mean the person he was; and the one he's become. Her, too. *That* foursome.

So it was with Eliza's parents.

Proof? It's everywhere, the proof of our astounding metamorphic capability. Except it's *not* "astounding," it's our first prenatal talent and we bear it all our years: we start as "stem cells," undifferentiated, each with the promise of specifying into, say, the isinglass rind of a toenail *or* the watt-charged web that lights the neocortex *or* the tiny museum of bones inside the ear *or* . . . well, or *anything* bodily human (or selectively pre-human: we're still things of gill and wing in the womb). It ought to be clear by the time the intrauterine photos show a fetus floating in its angelically silky hairshirt of lanugo: we were born to be to identity what the chameleon is to color.

And: "Canadian scientists grafted bits of human ovary tissue onto a mouse's muscles, then harvested usable eggs from the grafts, maturing them in a lab" (this, to explore the possibility of exo-womb fertility for "ovarian cancer patients or those with such conditions as endometriosis or lupus"). Proof that we're a fingersnap of cellgerm transposition away from such cross-species intimacy as would have left even Mendel and Darwin addle-eyed amid their specimen albums. But surely, now, the "weird" conversions of our old dorm-room compadres—stalwart atheist, to sober Roman Catholic; workaholic CEO, to gutter druggie—can be seen as just the somewhat all-too-gung-ho application of an everyday potential.[1]

We could say that the ligatured psyche of the carnival hermaphrodite Ed-Edna; and the physically elided lives of Siamese twins; and (whether fraud or genuine) the blended speech of medium-*cum*-channeled-"spirit-mentor" . . . are outlandish variations on the dialogues that we've all, in small ways, welcomed to our consciousness, that sometimes override us unexpectedly: the seepage of a chill, unreasoned sadness; or a woes-erasing wave of gratuitous grace.

"I was so far from wanting words, that I had only too many of them. I didn't know what to do with them. I floundered among them as if they were water which I was splashing about." Dickens had his hero report this somewhere amid the 8-to-900ish pages of *David Copperfield* (as if, perhaps, it applied to himself?) and then, in a stroke of what today we'd say was "metatextual gesture," he cut those words from the published version . . . a man of two minds. (A man, indeed, whose full *oeuvre*-tally of characters—"imaginary or real," as Norrie Epstein says in *The Friendly Dickens*—is *13,143:* imagine being the chosen census-taker in a brain like that.)[2]

The late-nineteenth-century visionary painter Albert Pinkham Ryder "has money—all the money he needs," as that pop-mystical writer Kahlil Gibran described him, and yet he dressed in grimy tatters and lived in a kind of eccentric austerity that bordered on other people's ideas of "filth" (the painter William H. Hyde said Ryder would frequently show up at art class "smelling of the stables"). And Gibran goes on to explain for us, "He is no longer on this planet. He is beyond his own dreams."

Well, what of a man whose calling isn't quite so superhuman? Can't he still encompass multiple worlds?—even if he's not a genius, even if his eyes don't have the inwardgazing fixity of Ryder's 1883 self-portrait. And in any case, Eliza would have gladly said at one time that her father *was* a genius, albeit not within the arts. She would have said the muses oversaw his scalpel with the same concern for burnishing fire and gravid weight they gave to Rembrandt's brush.

I once wrote a brief poem that incorporated a tree a friend of mine remembers from childhood. It was blasted into char by a dead-on lightning-strike. That's what they called it for many years, "the char tree." But later, after road expansion was approved by the city council, they needed to dig it up. It had harbored a secret life all along, of glass roots from the alchemical touch of the lightning blast: a gorgeous, vitrine jellyfish of roots no one had guessed at.

ꙮ

They required mastectomies. He was their doctor: young, but aura'd in ability and confidence; good-looking in a dewy way; and "sensitive," whatever that means, whatever exquisitude molecules comprise it. For over two generations, dreamyboy Hollywood actors had been playing at being physicians: they were due for a physician who resembled a dreamyboy Hollywood type. He loved his wife—the marriage wasn't a secret—and yet he kept the ring, a dazzling gold band, set around a collection vial he turned on its side each morning. There was something about this fiction—"availability"—that he knew was, in a manner unaccounted for by regulation medschool textbooks, therapeutic.

Randolph Phillips: I'd heard of him, a reputable but just *too* dashing "women's specialty" surgeon (early on, the usual spiteful rumors had started), before I ever became a close friend to his daughter Eliza.

"Doctor Smith" and "Doctor Jones," but always with him the first name, Doctor Randolph, as if this made a game of what was otherwise a matter of fear and hurt and disfigurement. This sprig of informality only further enabled the fantasy sense of flirtation, as with a certain kind of hairdresser and his clientele: *Girls! Mister Francis Is Back From Vacation!* First the nurses picked it up, and eventually his colleagues of both genders, and finally even the sterner bigwigs among the administrators—as if he had really become that creation. There was a night he arrived home from a late shift, Shelley opened the door in her look-it-still-fit-her honeymoon lingerie, and she rolled out her huskiest purr-voice: "Hey there, Doctor Randolph."

Not that I want to imply his surgical skill was second to his charisma. No; and even the standardly envious of his fellow surgeons—rumormongers, vilifiers, imams of the snide jibe on the putting green—confined their innuendo to personal matters. (Even "Heartache Jake," the world-class cardiologist and putz.) As for his steadiness of hand, his diagnostic expertise, and his unerring, creative forays into the sickly quick of flesh gone wrong . . . here, his most rabidly active detractors, even, needed (grudgingly) to yield to the opinion that "he makes it look as beautiful as ballet." "That boy could piss through the eye of a needle and never get it wet." "*Of course* he's good with cysts; the crazy fucker can *think like* a cyst." Plus, he was *serious;* beyond prestige and dollars, he'd declared a one-man holy war against the nation of tumors. He slipped into his white physician's smock as determinedly as someone else might don the black *gi* of a master of martial arts.[3]

Nor do I want to imply this was merely a lark for his patients, an excuse to play the femme fatale. Most were thoroughly terrified and were grateful for simple frankness and courtesy. Anything more on their own part, any eyelash-batted simpering or dove-coo double entendre, they could lavish on a handsome dermatologist, whose stakes for playing a round of infatuation were way, *way* lower.

The majority of what he endured in his office resembled less a romp from Boccaccio and more a newfound circle of hell that Dante had overlooked the first time, maybe because he couldn't comprehend such unjust punishment might be visited on sufferers whose sins, whatever they were, had no connection to the kind of news that Phillips was required to deliver. Smoking?—yes, the lungs. And sexual indiscretion?—STDs. But *this* discovery in the land of milk and natural pleasure . . . who *could* understand the body's own traitorous rampage? "Grow," "grown," "growing," all of those words were fine; but suddenly "growth" was in your doctor's mouth—"*a* growth," "*the* growth," "*your* growth," as if you'd gardened this monstrous death flower into existence—and everything under the harshly clinical light of his ceiling did a jittery jump cut into a future that, with a flicker of seconds, was removed from the ongoing stream of the past by a factor that could only be measured in units of skincrawl horror. "Removed": that, too, was a word with new gravity now.[4]

Reactions varied. Weeping itself occurred along a graded line. For some: a beast a thousand miles that long burst forth foaming from its insufficient cage and kept on pouring out, for hours. One woman shook herself around the room that way, as if a gang of invisible thugs repeatedly punched her. Sedatives didn't help. The orderlies held her down: she finally shrieked herself into unconsciousness. But others remained composed or even clearly made a fetish of composure, it was so dear an ideal. A few in his career had even sat there, listening quietly, drying an eye on occasion, shaping a cogent question: they achieved what diehard misanthropes would still have agreed was a dignity.

Others: anger. At him. At God. At their own impossible systems: one suburban matron started in on beating her chest with her small, prim fists so uncontrollably, the bruises reminded the staff of that grape-bunch purple they'd see across cardiac patients' sternums. Others: self-disgust. Yet others: automatic moans in the skyward direction of Jesus and Mary (one dropped to her knees in a badly misplaced tray of footbath fungicide). Perhaps, he thought, the saddest were the delusional: through torturous logic, this was "just what I needed," or this loss "will bring the family back together again," "renew my faltered faith," "serve as a rallying point," etc. Some believed they *deserved* it. Some vomited: so much for "composure."

A stripper had double-Deed herself with implants only a year before ("Believe me: you *don't want* to know what I had to do to afford them"), and she gripped the arms of his buttery leather patient's chair and cursed the curses of demonshit and pitfire down upon her own mother—presumably, for passing on the likelihood.[5] The worst, though, was the mother with the healthy, richly lifting bosom, clinging to her fifteen-year-old daughter—who'd soon be under his blade. *Take mine instead,* her eyes kept screaming, love, and guilt, and an agony only the truly damned know, *Let me give mine!*

Do videos help? Do 1-800 answer lines and neighborhood support groups? Yes no probably. But this all happened several cultural moments before such forward-thinking ablements were so commonplace. He picked up the slack. He carried the emotional hod. It wasn't any love cruise.

Still, those rumors. And his growly "bedroom voice." Eliza remembers overhearing her mother say to a friend, "I swear that some are happy for their cancer, to have an excuse to bask in his presence." Eliza was ten or so. She thought, then, it was a compliment.

"Shelley, that's cruel."

"Look, don't tell *me* what's cruel. *You* live with Mack the Knife for a dozen years and see how jolly it is." But at ten you're not hip to such cynicism.

Some of them hollered their grief so long, so rough, they wound up coughing blood. Some wept in a private circle of calm; or anyway, *relative* calm. Some asked what their husbands or lovers would feel. And could they still nurse with the one that was left? And could they . . . *you know* . . . ever again? Would they be attractive, ever again?

No wonder he had to comfort them.[6]

∽

In the Legion of Super-Heroes series of comic books, one member (maybe Cosmic Boy? or Saturn Girl? or Lightning Lad?—but it wasn't, I'm sure, the zeppelin-like, expandably spheroid Bouncing Boy) was often depicted with Proty, a blobbo extraterrestrial mascot, which was something like a living gooey football. Its power: it could reformat its body to look like *anything,* and credibly so: a leopard-bird from the swamps of Galaxy Seven, a vampire orchid from one of the Taboo Planets of Sirius. This helped out in a number of plot contrivances; and between its calls to action, Proty, as I remember, was otherwise found demurely perched on a Legionnaire's shoulder or happily squirming its way across the ground.

This notion of abracadabra corporeal change is common enough in the universe of adolescent fancy. Rick Starr (aka Space Ranger) was often accompanied in his rocket cruiser, The Solar King, by not only perky blond secretary Myra, but by his infini-elastically transshaping alien buddy, the webbed and tootle-nosed Cryll ("I've changed into a NEPTUNIAN ELECTRIC EEL—and can absorb electricity as a sponge absorbs water!"—although he includes, in the same adventure, "The Great

Plutonium Plot" in *Showcase* of August 1958, this sensible self-delimitation: "I only do it for laughs . . . or to help YOU, Space Ranger!").

He's bubblegum pink, and round, and doughily simple of line and detail, and he really *does* look like a slightly lighter version of the deep pink embryonic stem cells featured on the cover of a *Newsweek* (July 9, 2001). His flexuous ability to morph *(zing!)* into a 7-story-tall Uranian wormbeast or the lovely Tiger of Paradise from one of Jupiter's moons is just a wackier extension of those cells' "pluripotent ability to differentiate into any of the 220 cell types that make a human body, from the kidney and heart and liver to the skin, neuronal and pancreatic. For a few short days they are blank slates waiting for destiny (or the complex interplay of genes and biochemistry) to write their future." *Zing,* indeed.

Two hundred and twenty. That truth of our earliest in-womb selves makes laughable the supposedly impressive power of teenage Legionnaire Triplicate Girl (a *tri*partite body? *three?* Ho-hum). And the whole of our species history is enough to beggar the most extreme of Cryll's and Proty's switch-o, change-o guises—I mean back to the original dot when space and time were one, and then the Bang, and then the elements, the elements of *everything,* from methane ice in Saturn's rings, to the pollen-dusted tuft of a bee; from crusts that ride the here-then-not-here surfaces of suns, to the brain that houses the mind of a man in his office slamming the door on the woes and the winks of doctor-him, and readying to be daddy-him and husband-him for the scant hours left of his wakefulness.[7]

☙

Some days it happened as casually as entering a plane in East Coast time and then exiting Central; he was Doctor Randolph and one easy half-hour ride away he wasn't, he was asking Eliza how was her day at preschool, honey. Oh, maybe a little distracted, sure, but that wore off in a while, or what's the sapphire heart of a gin-and-tonic *for?*

On other days, though, he would need to repeatedly *force* the Ran-man's afternoon of consultations back into its proper partitioned-off space. He pictured himself with a whip and a jungle beast—or no, a wooden stake and a ghoulish thing, an unspeakable thing, that refused to remain in its coffin.

So when Shelley opened the door that night in her wafting peekaboo flimsies, that was fine—hey, that was *very* fine. But then she purred her "Hey there, Doctor Randolph"—and it was untenable, it undid the division he'd labored so hard to construct . . . construct for *her* sake, to protect her from the rigors of his workday. Didn't she *see* that, goddamit? Didn't she see how that linking she'd made was unholy, goddamit? "Goddamit," he said and went out to the yard in a sudden sullen mood, which wasn't what he'd intended at all and wasn't what she'd intended—standing there now alone in the hall in her swirl of smoky bedtime petals—at all, at all.

⌒

As the years passed, it became second nature. There were two of him, Ran-man the Great and House Man. That's the superhero way in which he thought of it, *when* he thought of it, which was increasingly seldom. Eliza could tell: what she had for herself was only a piece of her father; and, as she began to comprehend the import of his work, that image mixed itself with a vision of floating body parts across the heavens . . . bra-cup balls of flesh that were tipped with ruby nipples . . . sawed-off, stingy slices of her parents' invaluable time. . . . "And so my therapist said I started pretty early seeing life as essentially fractured—seeing my task in life as 'seeking out unification.'"

Okay; sure. Although who *doesn't* undergo a childhood deeply structured by minute-to-minute dualities? In Sheldon Mayer's savvy 1950s–60s comic-book series *Sugar and Spike,* the two eponymous toddlers are always drawn full-figure, and shown to the reader straight-on from their own floor-level point of view. The adults are invariably drawn from the knees down only, so at once are given an air of unreachable loftiness *and* a sense of having become inconsequential: those legs mean little more than "background"—weather on far-off hills— until, like a storm come in from those hills, a spanking arrives to enliven the story. (In Schulz's comic strip *Peanuts,* of course, the grown-ups *never* appear, not one admonishing finger of them.)

Kenneth Grahame's late-Victorian childhood reminiscences in *The Golden Age* describe a similar two-tracked world: one's playfriends and the towering others: "On the whole, the existence of these Olympians seemed to be entirely void of interests, even as their movements were confined and slow, and their habits stereotyped and senseless. It was incessant matter for amazement how these Olympians would talk over our heads—during meals, for instance—of this or that social or political inanity, under the delusion that these pale phantasms of reality were among the importances of life. This strange anaemic order of beings was further removed from us, in fact, than the kindly beasts who shared our natural existence in the sun."

When my friends Monica and Michael were out in the yard last month with Guthrie, two years old, they found the carcass of a bird (already partly chewed at its fringes). Monica lifted it with a garden spade and, Guthrie following (silent, wide-eyed), deposited it in the trash can. Now these friends of mine don't drag God into their child raising; even so, they both want Guthrie to understand that neighbors he'll meet do hold religious beliefs; and thus, next day at rest time, his mother explained, "Guthrie . . . you know, some people would say when an animal dies— like yesterday, the bird—or also when people die, they go Somewhere Better." At which, Guthrie set his Thomas the toy train down, considered his mother for a moment with stern appraisal, and then, attempting to disabuse her of her benightedness as gently as he might, said, "Momma? *Dat* bird in da trash."—already learning to weave, unweave, and reweave antipodal realms.

Or can't the brush of duality tint us earlier, even, than Guthrie's age? Australia's *Gold Coast Bulletin* reports the two-year-old Chinese boy who, after complaining of a stomachache, was hospitalized in Heilongjiang Province Hospital and diagnosed as having "the fist-sized foetus of his twin still lodged in his abdomen."

⌒

"Well Albert, *yes* I know that everybody feels *some* kind of doubleness, or more. I mean I *know* you're not the same, let's say, in front of a class as you are with your friends. I mean—makeup, for chrissake, that's what

makeup is: a separate face.[8] But I'm talking about"—
this is drink-three time—"I was seriously obsessive-
compulsive back then."

"Like how?" It's interesting: some bars are pretty
claustrophobic places, not large, and often crowded,
often filled with smoke and smell and blather that make
the walls seem all the closer. Even so, when someone
opens up, as now, with Eliza . . . when the stories behind
the stories appear . . . a spaciousness occurs (a priest
might say the same of a confessional booth) and in
human-life units it's *miles* to the horizon.

"Like making a hundred lists a day. Of food I had in
the refrigerator. But then if I had cheese, I might write
Havarti and start a separate list for 'h' foods whether I
had them or not, or it might go under 'd' for *Danish,* or
both.[9] I really *do* think it all came from my father. I did a
long list of synonyms for tits once."[10]

"And you thought that . . . what? . . . this would make
your life whole again?"

"If I had enough lists. If I had *every* list, I would have
the whole world, without gaps.[11] You see?—my parents
led me, none of it intentional, but they led me to feel that
people meant gaps. My therapist said that this explains
my own divorce, and why I loved astronomy so early. I
made lists of stars, like my heroes did. I wanted big theo-
ries that unified."

"But you're better now."

"Well now, yeah. *That* way. Even so, an incomplete
thing, like an incomplete sentence?—it drives me cray-
ZEE!"

"I'd guess, however. . . ."

"What?"

"Oh . . . nothing."

"Right. *Très* ha-ha funny."

⌢

He smelled of the stables. . . .

It only made sense: if you needed to paint them, you needed to know them. Sometimes he'd sleep there—losing the human, individual edge of himself in the larger, absorbent, dark atmosphere that the straw and the wood and the breathing of the horses contributed to.

In Albert Pinkham Ryder's 1870s painting, *In the Stable,* the white horse, on its shadowy background, tells us that its heavy and complex body—all of the tight-packed equine musculature and its architecture of bone and nerve—can still have the quick, lyric feel of chalk dust blown, as if almost by accident, into the shape of a horse on a blackboard. ("A glistening, almost phosphorescent body," Davidson says in his critical appreciation.)

This is true as well of his later painting, *The White Horse:* something spectral, aerial, philosophical yearns to rise like a willowy exit of flume from this creature with its four legs that are otherwise planted as solidly on the ground as a Mennonite dinner table . . . as if we witness the poolball-atom solids of Newtonian physics suddenly, before our eyes, receiving a prescient glimmer of the iffier, quarkier quasi-things they'll be in the coming century.[12]

Ryder's life, as we've seen, underwent this same milky split: his visions rising like cream to the top of a daily existence that, left unattended, seemed little more to the world than old whey souring in the heat.[13] He slept on three chairs draped in old clothes. Visitors were appalled by the stench—and even so, "He makes me ashamed of being clean," said Kahlil Gibran. Rheumy of eye, smutty of dress, and crabbed of gait by the end of his life (Gibran again: "He takes steps about two inches long"), Ryder managed to send up a tendril—rooted in the benches of tramps and the muckpiles of the paddocks—that, at its higher end, achieved a grip on the windowsill to infinity.

And Eliza . . . ? In a universe of schism *that* severe, she needed to "seek out unification," to be a bridger of rifts.

"When I was fourteen, I started on my haphazard trips through astronomy: a teacher gave me some books. I already loved reading. You can imagine from what I've told you: all of my books lined up by size, from shirt-pocket Biblical tracts to trendy hairstyle books as large as newspaper pages. And then I'd try to get doubles so I could arrange them by color of spine as well. Or by author—see?—if I had, like, J, K, L, M, N, O, Q, I'd be frantic until I could find an appropriate P.

"That's what happened. This teacher gave me a book by Cecilia Payne. Or really Cecilia Payne-Gaposchkin, after she married. Do you know what a 'computer' was back then, say 1920?"

"No . . . *yes!* The women who compiled massive catalogues of stars for the hotshot astronomers—right?"

"Right. Gruntwork. But of course I *loved* the idea: lists! Of stars! And Payne has *beautiful* persuasive prose on the elemental consistency of the universe—if the elements are here on Earth, they're Out There in the stars as well. There's no real gap, on *that* level. For me . . . well, you can see the appeal."

"The way that airports are these days, and fast-food restaurants. No matter how far we go, we're at home."

"Yeah." [pause] "But . . . more exalting."

A horse that flimmers connectively into the air—the way the ocean also does, in Ryder's seascapes.

⌒

A fifteenth-century Spanish or Portuguese Catholic convert, made of a Jew—in a time when a Jew converted with the encouragement of his wrists in chains and a man with an iron-tipped club above him. In fancier cases, there was also the eye gouge and the heated brand and a chance to contribute one's tongue to a collection nailed onto the wall.

And some of these converts rose to lives of esteem in the Spanish kingdoms—here a minister, there a judge, a rector, a bishop—and some no doubt were sincere in their crosstheology, why not? Once a God has allowed your seeing your mother bound in rope and her thumbs smashed flat, it's hard to feel loyalty. Still others, at the risk of similar torture, only converted in surface ritual: their earlier faith they carried inside, a secret seed in a deeply buried secret garden, tended to covertly. Whispers. Initiate signs.

Marrano, they were called: pig. Another bifurcated life.[14]

Is this how her father saw his compartmented self? Victim, hero, bearer of an unknown alternate Randolph Phillips?

Hero, certainly. And he did intend the best for his family, at least at the first, when he'd reasoned it out. He thought of it not as prohibiting their engagement with his professional life, but more as his protecting them from every pissy two-bit horror unleashed from the pits of oncology. He'd shoulder this burden alone. He may have flirted at times with the adjective "noble." He may have seen himself playing himself in the movie version.

The way Shelley saw it . . . ? One afternoon she was treating herself to a lemon cake and a merlot at The Grapevine with her friend Giselle. Well, four merlots, if you want the truth; four in hasty succession.

"Shelley, don't be so picky you pick it to death. I love you like a sister, girl, but I gotta tell you, they *all* come with baggage. So? So he has baggage. Plenty of women in this town call him Captain Perfecto."

"Right. And I'm Lois Lane." She studied some far-away cloud-land at the center of her wine. This would have been around when Eliza was ten. The first of the pressure cracks starting to show.

"I'm Lois Lane and every night I get *two* stinking hours with Clark Kent, while the rest of the world gets *fourteen* goddam fucking hours of Superman."

∽

Another bifurcated life: the Cubano oncologist. Tire-rafted off from the Havana coast and met his connection a couple of miles out. Is now a janitor in an Athens, Georgia hospital. The first half of his life having seemingly melted in the sea.

Another bifurcated life: the Cubano shit-for-brains street thief. Is now a realtor in the L.A. hills: mistress, butler, political strings.

Another: the stripper, the Ran-man's angry patient (Dakota). Is also a Ph.D. in economics student (Tammani). Is also a single mother (Mommy). It won't stop, it goes on, on, on: "bifurcation" doesn't come *close*. ("Silly cones," her daughter calls them: cute. One day she had to

respond, "Hey: I'm going to be a unicone": cute, with a
soupçon of acid.)

I think *Moby-Dick* is that very rare thing, inarguable
genius; and even so, its characters don't ring "true"—at
least, they don't ring fully round. Ishmael goes from
nothing more complex than chafing inwardly to sniff the
ocean's intimate folds, *bingo,* to having his wish fulfilled.
That any pregnant woman or ex-employer or bill collector or fellow whittler-of-decoy-ducks might have a claim
on him, and so imply a range of Ishmaelness untapped
by the daily demands of a whaler's routine . . . is never
even hinted at; and so, on the whole, for the rest of the
crew: who follow like cork chips floating in the wake of
Ahab's searing, atemporal monomania. It's gripping and
poetic prose, yes; but my enemies and friends are people,
not allegories.

By age sixteen, Eliza was coming increasingly to see
that it wasn't a hallmark of only the Phillipses' psyches:
everyone was an X on a graph, and could just as easily be
X-7 or X-9 tomorrow, depending on who-knows-*what*-
unprophesiable-throw-of-a-pair-of-invisible-dice.[15]

"Sixteen: the hormones didn't help. To be [*stage whisper:*] a virgin or not to be [*stage whisper:*] a virgin—*that*
question, and all of the similar high-school-age baloney."
Other girls were hotties one day, icicles the next: "Not
even menstrual craze accounts for periodicity like that."
And the boys?—"Dr. Jekyll and Mr. Crap. Their personalities switched gears with more speed than their com-
plexions, and *that's* saying something. If only they'd been
bitten by werewolves—which would have seemed interesting. But they were bitten by werejerks, and it didn't require a full moon: any sixty watts could bring it on." The

teachers, too: the rumors about Ms. Santo's private life, etc. [More on that, upcoming.] Late one afternoon they found Eliza mesmerized in front of a girl's-room mirror; everyone else had languidly left the john at the blat of the three-o'clock bell. She wasn't crying, wasn't applying lip gloss, wasn't smearing zit cream over recent needle tracks: "I only stood there . . . it was maybe fifteen minutes until they ushered me out . . . lost in the realization that *Eliza Phillips wasn't exempt:* I was standing there looking to see how many mes I could find in the mirror."[16]

That's when the therapy began, and when her interest in astronomy achieved the zealous intensity of totem worship. "I carried her, Cecilia Payne, around in my mind like some carved rock of a deity I was forbidden by holy law to ever set down for a minute." Even now, as Eliza's idly twisting paper napkins and shredded tinfoil while she speaks—the way we all do, if we're nervous—she looks as if she might be trying to iconically shape an abstract representation of her hero.

"That was around the time the Shelley shit was hitting the Randolph fan big-time—she'd discovered his secret appointment book by then, the one I told you about; so Payne and her sense of the sky—or really *my* sense of her sense of the sky—was a security I clung to. All of the ways we order randomness up there—a Belt, a Dipper, Fishes, you know—and all of the regimented spectra lines that Payne investigated, these things said there were parts of the universe I could count on not to change unrecognizably the moment I turned my back. It's nuts but, like, when I'm shopping at Food-4-Less and the cashier lifts some product with a bar code? . . . I get a sweet feeling inside. It looks to me like the spectra lines for elements in the composition of stars that Payne was so extraordinarily devoted to.

"Look." She snaps a few of our drinkery's cheap toothpicks into nearly-but-not-wholly separated halves; arrays them on the table in a specific party-trick pattern; and then drips a couple of beads of gin and tonic (number four by now) into the center of this. It flowers: the shape of a five-point star.

"I wanted *all* of the stars to be like that: at my command, and never failing.

"Anyway, by the time my parents divorced, when I was eighteen, I declared my major: astronomy. I thought it would save me. Both of them left the house, they simply *gave* it to me, and so I stayed there, feeling . . . because it always occurred in the terms of my father's practice, okay? . . . *amputated* from something I'd originally been a part of.[17]

"You know 'phantom limb'?—when the body continues to feel sensation as if its severed leg or arm were still attached? Well, nobody ever wonders if the chopped-off *body part* still feels anything, but I can tell you: yes it does, its nerve ends burn in the bed at night like a million oil refineries seen from an airplane.

"We had that little garden in back, some morning glory, peppers, potatoes . . . Payne had started out with an interest in botany, and so *of course* I'd made a little green plot in our yard. Payne married a Russian, *I* married a Russian: poor Jay never understood he was only being used for my copycat purposes. Not that *I* understood it either, not at the time—where was I?"

"The garden?"

"Oh yeah, the garden. You've seen it."

"You've lived there . . . what? ten years now?"

"Going on ten. My parents left, Jay left . . . but I'm there. Not as confused, though, as I was at eighteen. I'd walk out into the garden at dusk, covering" [she demonstrates] "my own poor widdle 32-A toodles in my hands as if *some* Surgeon of the Gods was due to come and try to sever them from my body—like, symbolic proof that I was just a leftover piece of my parents' failed marriage.

"I guess it was all about me. It wasn't a 'divorce.' They'd had an Elizaectomy."

. . . walking out of the lights of the kitchen, into the complicated grays and deepening lavenders of the backyard air at eight or nine o'clock, with nothing on her but a negligee of shadows, with her hands like insufficient shields against what Life can do to a life.

࿇

Another bifurcation: "I was able to preserve my great brain from the influence of my sexual instinct, so that I coupled passionately, and thought lucidly all the time— and then I wrote!" (August Strindberg).

Those artsy types are chockablock with dividedness. Another one: "God forgive me, I do still see that my nature is not to be quite conquered, but will esteem pleasure above all things; music and women I cannot but give way to, whatever my business is" (Samuel Pepys).[18]

Another: Ishmael and Queequeg. Melville makes of them strange scrambled-image brothers, of a mystically nonsanguinary but soulfully tethered kind. (Some say nonphysical but soulfully tethered lovers is also a possible reading; or, between the lines, physical lovers, too.)

One of the novel's many iterations of this duo is that moment when the "vast corpse" of a successfully hunted whale is chained to the Pequod: "Tied by the head to the stern, and by the tail to the bows, the whale now lies with its black hull close to the vessel's, and seen through the darkness of the night, the two—ship and whale—seemed yoked together like colossal bullocks, whereof one reclines while the other remains standing."

Then the knives come out. *Moby-Dick* reads like a survey of (or paean to?) dismemberments—if one perceives its cosmos through the eyes of Eliza in dismemberment mode. "At times, when closely pursued, [the spermaceti whale] will disgorge what are supposed to be the detached arms of the squid; some of them thus exhibited exceeding twenty and thirty feet in length." Presumably, Ahab's other leg may once have been a minor contribution to such upheaved gastrojecta.

"Every sailor a butcher."[19] Ishmael, in the instructive chapter titled "Cutting In": "In the case of a small Sperm Whale the brains are accounted a fine dish. The casket of the skull is broken into with an axe, and the two plump, whitish lobes being withdrawn . . . ," etc. Everything, everyone, is liable to separation ("Killed and hoisted on deck for the sake of his skin, one of these sharks almost took poor Queequeg's hand off, when he tried to shut down the dead lid of his murderous jaw"). We remember that sailors *are* "hands" ("All hands report on deck!"). By novel's end, just one hand—Ishmael—is left floating in the waves: a floating limb, of what was once a living communal body of men. But at the end, as that body goes down, he (and he alone) is disgorged.[20]

And Albert Pinkham Ryder's *Jonah* recreates its Old Testament chestnut turbulently, in bilious chartreuse pinnacles and nadirs of water, with God looking down at this bit of His nasty handiwork from an operatically cumulonimbus sky. The critic Abraham Davidson: "I can think of nothing in nineteenth-century American painting that can be called visionary . . . that contains at the same time as much awesome grandeur." He also suggests that Ryder may have seized upon this subject from "its version in the form of a sermon put by Melville in the mouth of Father Mapple in chapter 9 of *Moby-Dick.*"

There's no proof for that tempting theory, but the novel was already forty years in the world by the time of Ryder's painting. Surely Melville would have understood how Ryder has fashioned a whale "shaped curiously like the ship with its terrified occupants."—Just as Eliza understands the double-level universe depicted in Ryder's *Jonah,* a duality of human strife and great deific distance. "Fractions. Mommy and Daddy. Secret life and home life. Them and me." An accurate map of existence—*if* we perceive it through eyes in dismemberment mode. "*No wonder* Jay claimed I was weirder by the month. I found it hard to believe he would come home after two hours of rush-hour traffic and be the same person who'd started out. *Two hours!* Hell, my father had witnessed people's lives completely change in only two *seconds* of X-ray analysis.

"The thing is, though . . . I could also get high on this scary perception. I worked to defeat it—that's what Payne and celestial data were all about—but I liked it, too. It was exhilarating."

We've wisely enough declared a fresh-air break between drinks four and five. Outside, on the street-front deck, a little war goes on: lingeringly late honeysuckle versus the blossoms of car exhaust. We sit at a railside table and study this evening's revelers strolling on past. I've known Eliza now for seven years. Just after she and Jay split up, she entered one of my readings courses; even though her major wasn't lit, she was clearly the brain in the room with the keenest cutting edge . . . perhaps a metaphor I automatically worked up having learned whose daughter she was. Since then, I've followed Eliza through two jobs, into the gym-pumped arms of current sweetie C., and up and down the steps of several therapists' offices. Usually, zippy chitchat. Not tonight, however.

"You know *Our Mutual Friend?* Dickens?"

"That's right . . . it was on the syllabus." We watch a woman walk the block: puddle of bar-light, darkness, puddle of bar-light, darkness, puddle . . . as if she's telling beads, but on a scale of city planning. "There's that scene where a man who was drowned in the Thames is revived. It's *so* fucking powerful."

"And . . . ?"

"And Dickens even uses, I remember after all these years, the phrase 'the living-dead man.' I mean, the scene is ghastly in so many ways, but I remember thinking: Wow! A man who'd been in two worlds as completely unattached as Life and Death! It seemed so ideal to me. I don't mean I was suicidal, far from it: I felt more alive than ever. Sort of as if . . . in *admitting* these gaps we all of us stumble through . . . if you *truly admit* them, you carry a charge across the gaps! Sometimes, in those days,

I was very depressed; but other times, I tingled all over, I
had this special vision of things. My power: *I was aware of
the gaps.*[21]

"You understand? It was a secret vision. The more it
was secret, kept away from everyone, on its own side of a
gap, the more the vision was true. The more it was true,
the more I kept it my secret. Those were heady times.

[pause]

"But I much prefer being sane now."

⌣

And across the street, that woman retraces her steps: a
small oasis of light, the dark, a small oasis of light . . .
until she disappears off the edge of the last of the spots of
light as if off the edge of the world, and so is fully ab-
sorbed by the darkness.

Properly enough, as she's a stranger to me. She's returned to the wilds of strangerhood—yet *another* locus on
the farther side of one of Eliza's seemingly endless series
of "gaps."

Properly *and* thankfully enough, for I can't concentrate
just now on more than Eliza herself: an extra person's
cargo of Mardi Gras pleasures or slithering silverfish
horrors *surely* would be psycho-intake overload resulting
in Albert meltdown.

Farewell, stranger lady.

A fleeting thought, however . . . in addition to his
wife, his children, actress-lover, hangers-on, editorial colleagues, various fellow gallivanters, publishers, navvies,
royalty, bootblacks, political cronies, butler, maid, and
the rest of his life's compendium of other actual lives . . .
in addition, Dickens's head held 13,143 people, in a paral-

lel dimension that he folded small and carried about in a mental Gladstone bag in his brain.

The very *thought* of it suddenly makes my head so heavy, I need to rest it in both of my opened hands—a child who's just discovered that the bowling ball he chose from the rack is . . . really . . . a . . . bit . . . too . . . much . . . for . . . him.

⌒

It won't stop, it goes on, on, on . . . if we look through dismemberment eyes. It starts the moment the umbilicus is snipped . . . the sleek bean astronaut is banished from his lifeline to the mother ship . . . the gate to his holistic time in Eden is forever barred in flaming seraph-swords . . .

. . . and it won't end until the soul at last is tricked out through a pore by Death's efficient, microfilamental hook.[22]

In one medieval painting I've always found to be forceful, this idea of separation is presented as a fresh corpse on a table covered in—softened by—richly burgundy tapestry; above it, the departed spirit (precisely the size and shape of the body, except it's the texture of honey or pus) still hovers for a second, not yet budded off completely, but attached where the spirit touches its lips to the lips of its twin, the cadaver.

For this second: they kiss like gourami.

⌒

Randolph Phillips performing an operation. This time, though, I don't mean the elliptical incision around the nipple and the biopsy scar; and a peeling back of that skin; and then the slicing away of the relevant tissue from out of its home between the ribs and the collarbone, between the side and the sternum; not the "simple," not the "modified radical," not the "radical." ("Simple"!— *try* that out on the mother who's watching her fifteen-year-old daughter wheeled down the hall on a gurney, out of the land of the blessedly intact.)[23]

But no; this time, I merely mean the sushi-chef finesse with which he supplely disengages the life he can freely talk about with his family, from the life—an hour here, two hours there—of his more furtive strings of intrigues. He needed to comfort them, he told himself, to stroke the trepidation very gradually out of those lovely, needy, stricken hillocks of womanly flesh. The way some kinds of panic stiffen nipples as surely as sexual excitation. The beautiful vale between. He was lost. He kept two sets of appointment books (*good book, bad book*) the way, we know, Columbus kept two captain's logs on the first of his voyages, one of actual reckonings and fears, and another—this one, his adept "disinformation log"—of doctored (and therefore cheerier) stats intended to appease the fractious tempers of his crew as the stores of rat-shat hardtack ran low, and the lash was employed, and the sea-beasts of the outer reaches were witnessed at night keeping pace with the ships, a promise of terrible penance for their trespass into the Ocean Unknown.

("Doctored"—for *our* purposes, a gratifying way of saying "falsified.")

And where, when, did the ethos of an innocently gridded personality (let's see . . . home life, *here;* office tumult, *over here;* dark wanderings of the mind, *up there* . . .) allow for the likely (and yet, of course, not *necessary*) next step, which is counting on those grid walls to conceal the prohibited? Phillips couldn't say. For anyone, how does it *ever* begin? ("No one was quite willing to lie, but they tugged down the edges of the truth"—Ann Patchett, in her novel *Bel Canto*.) "The slippery slope," my friends would probably call it; which of us *can* recognize the individual choices that elide to make its one slick, irresistible surface? "Slippery slope?" Eliza once said. "He was *king* of the downhill racers."[24]

If Columbus could . . . why shouldn't a surgeon working at Amity General?

If "a Buddhist monk in Thailand, Lim Laungpau, was arrested for fooling thousands of people into believing a hen had laid a golden egg" (they handed over huge donations, asking the hen—or the egg; it's not clear—to provide them with winning lottery numbers) . . . why not Doctor Randolph's small and harmless—yes, if undetected, harmless—series of gridded deceits?

If the owners of ancient Roman *popinae* watered their customers' wine.

Or worse, as the physician Galen accuses, served up "human flesh as pork."

If the blackbirds of England have been imitating car alarms.

And after all, his love for his wife was real: *that* wasn't at issue.

If the mummy that duped the experts. If the made-in-Hong-Kong Swiss watch. If the U.S. Senator under oath.[25]

"Hey, Ranner. We're getting ready to leave."

"What?" He looked up. "Oh, hiya, Heartache. 'Leave'?"

"My man, it's Friday. Three o'clock. You, me, Chuck,

Acey, Nguyen, Farker: drinks at the inn: every week: a tradition: hellOOOOO." This last through cupped hands, megaphonewise.

"I'm sorry, Heartache. Too much work. How's Millie?"

"Fine."

"And Vernon?"

"Fine."

"He's a good boy you've got there."

"Ranner . . . are you joining us or not?"

"I just can't, buddy. Not this week. Next Friday, I'll be good for it. Really."

"Okay then. And Ranner . . . none of my business, but . . . can't you have a *receptionist* keep your appointment book?"

"Oh. Usually, sure, but. . . ."

"See ya." And Jake was out of there.

If the forgery of a Shakespeare play. If the cup of placebo medicine. If the still leaf that's a mantis. If the life of counterfeit orgasms.

In the good book he wrote: *Drinks with the guys.*

He wrote in the bad book: *Sarah G.,* and closed it, and left by the side door.

‿

And as early as the first century, Pliny the Elder is associating physicians with a vigorous list of ethical transgressions, including adultery: "Of medical men, Vettius Valens was infamous for his affair with Messalina, wife of the Emperor Claudius.[26] Also the case of Eudemus with Livia, the wife of Drusus Caesar."

There's not much room, however, for squeamishness or shock in a work as compendious as Pliny's *Natural History.*

That lives are not reductive things, not seamless, mono-dimensional things, is a tacitly accepted understanding.

"Beyond the Nasamones, but near their borders, Calliphanes locates the Machlyes: they are bisexual and assume the role of either sex in intercourse. Aristotle adds that their right chest is that of a man, their left a woman's."

And: "It is not a myth that women have changed into men. The historical records show that during the consulship of Publius Licinius Crassus and Gaius Cassius Longinus, a girl at Casinum turned into a boy before her parents' very eyes."

There's no one only way to see the world, or be seen *by* the world. As symbol of this, we need only consider "the families practicing witchcraft among the Triballi and the Illyrians. Each of their eyes has two pupils."[27]

⌒

The note was brief, anonymously "written," and secretly slipped inside the slot. This was right before home computers: the letters were scissored from magazine-display type, like the parody of a ransom note . . . a joke.

Except it wasn't a joke. Shelley recognized that immediately.

YOURE HUSBAND IS HAVING AFAIRS WITH NURSES PATIENS MORE! DONT BELEVE ME?? GO TO OFFICE SEE S*E*C*R*E*T APOINTMINT BOOK!

A fellow doctor. She *knew* that. The misspellings were just too, *too* good.

She phoned Giselle that afternoon.

"Hey, Earth to Shelley: it's *not* a surprise. So? The eagle has landed. So what?"

"I'd prefer to use 'weasel.'"

"Look, I know you're angry . . ."

"I threw my wedding ring out the back window, into the garden."

". . . but okay, he's *not* Mr. Innocent. *Nor,* by the way, are *you* Mrs. Virgin Olive Oil, if you catch my drift. So? Life goes on, alimony goes on."

"I'm not sure I'm *that* angry yet."

"The timing is good, Shel. You're still hot enough to scorch some CEO or lawyer out there. Eliza is old enough to understand and to weather the cloudbursts.—Meet me in an hour, in the Amity west-side lobby."

"What?"

"We're going up to Randolph's office. Then I'm inviting him down to the cafeteria for a cup of coffee . . . a friend of mine, a node, see? Free advice. He'll do it, he's always been a sucker for doing favors. I'll coo like a dove. Sweet jezus, I'm a friend of his *wife's,* of *course* he'll spend a half hour lecturing me. And his wife is going to lag behind in his office and go through a few bottom drawers."

"Girl, for a PTA president, you sure come up with some crazyass shit."

She resisted at first. It was screwball. By the end, though, to the astonishment of neither, she complied. That's how easy it was. The two books were identical on the outside: a serious, wine red leather. Inside, one was rooted to the hour-by-hour overseeing of verifiable surgeries and consultations, seminars, endless skirmishes (some won, some not) with death. The other book?—its list of women's names was something that seemed to her to be afloat in a make-believe sky of its own, without a single tendril of connection along which *her* world's rules—the real world, as she thought of it—could travel and apply themselves. She suddenly saw how it was for him: he hadn't committed adultery. "Adultery" wasn't a concept in the insular world of these pages.

She used his own office phone to call an attorney.

⌒

"She may not have known I was home. I had just returned from school for the summer, and our schedules weren't yet very established. Not that I think it would have mattered, this wasn't an anger she could have controlled.

"She read a slip of paper. I didn't *know* what it was; but then again, this didn't require a shaman's intuition. I wasn't *stupid* about their marriage.

"She walked with great deliberation to the back room, took the gold ring off her finger, and pitched it into the yard as if she thought it had a chance of going into orbit around the Earth.[28]

"I think I hated her then. I'm not sure why—I mean, *she* was the one who felt betrayed. And yet it seemed so swift, and so one-way. And, Albert . . . she wasn't an angel, you know. Did she ask my advice, did she care at all that *I'd* be ripped in half at their divorce? And so I felt betrayed, too: only by her, not him.

"Man, they went *at* it that night! They didn't care *who* heard: me, neighbors, God Almighty: they might have heard it in China, I thought.

"I wasn't in the house, though. I was in the garden, on hands and knees, with a flashlight. Don't even ask me why; it's not as if I thought I'd find the ring and it would reunite them. I didn't plan on pawning it, or saving it for posterity, or . . . I don't know, exactly.[29] But I didn't want another incomplete thing in my life, another tangent line. I wanted that ring to come back. I wanted *one* thing to survive this wreck.[30]

"Well, it didn't. I stayed in the garden all night, I fell asleep holding the flashlight. When I walked back into the house, it was empty. I could feel the after-anger rico-cheting off the walls.

"I was filthy. I took a bath: a *long* bath, with all of the jasmine therapy stuff that my mother kept in little expen-sive gewgaw jars. And this I'll always remember: I stepped out of the tub, and toweled myself dry, and then I walked into their bedroom. I lay down in their bed.

"The echoes of them. . . . It made me feel dirtier than when I'd woke up in the garden."

‿

"Albert, I *agree:* I was loony, okay, I agree: like a little ani-mal out in the garden, sifting the guck a half an inch at a time. But that ring . . . it was my grandmother's, it was my birthright . . . I'd have gone and sifted Yosemite if I'd had to."

And we *do* obsess at the brink of the rift: how, how, how to suture it back to a Pangeatic wholeness?

NOCIRC, NORM, NO-HARMM, BUFF, UNCIRC, DOC—all, "foreskin restoration organizations."[31] As of millennial year 2000, they claim 20,000 men (the tempta-tion is "members") are proceeding with "stretching" by one technique or another, in an attempt to reclaim their amputated hoods. In his article about these groups, "The Foreskin Saga," John Sedgwick says the "frenar band" is "the ring of flesh that gives an uncircumcised foreskin its pucker." There are endless understandings of "birth-right." There are many kinds of rings; and each—what object *doesn't?*—holds inside of itself the possibility of its loss.

Not unexpectedly, the metaphor of "ring" for the cir-cumference-skin of the cock is ancient. Following the mass circumcision of Jewry at the end of the forty years of desert trekking (none had been performed in those decades of difficult journeying), the campsite where this holy rite took place "was thereafter known as *Gilgil,* the 'circle,' in allusion to the denuded corona and the circu-lar scar of circumcision."[32]

Sedgwick presents us with Chris, who "began by at-taching what little free skin he retained postcircumcision to an elastic band that ran down his leg, swinging once around his knee and clipping to his sock. He still wears this contraption every day, all day long, to tug him gently, to return him to what he once was and, he believes, what he should be." R. Wayne Griffiths moved from tape to "a pair of stainless-steel ball bearings—one an inch in diameter, the other an inch and a quarter—to dangle off himself."

This is principle and rage, not simple quirkiness. Eliza would understand. In fact, she's read the same article. I might have guessed; she's made herself an expert, from the ravages of Alzheimer's disease to the mystery dis-appearance behind those mateless socks we've all un-comprehendingly fished from the dryer. She's my Freud, Foucault, Maimonides of loss.

And Sedgwick says: "To them circumcision is a ques-tion neither of health nor of looking like Dad. It is a

matter of inalienable human rights, just as female circumcision is." Since we're talking about what's still the
most frequent surgical procedure for men in this country,
the oomph of the rhetoric employed is sometimes that of
a minority waging *jihad*. Sedgwick's article quotes Marilyn Milos, cofounder of NOCIRC: "Circumcised men
have been primally wounded, tortured and mutilated
when too little to defend themselves, and the best part of
their penis has been thrown into the trash can."

Of course, we all know scads of men who'd *never* want
that "droopy dewlap" (so goes one friend's estimation),
and a multitude of ditto-minded women who'd refuse to
harbor any of the unclipped, no matter how otherwise al-
luring. Health, aesthetics, scripture: manifold reasons.
The acrimony can wear deep chasms: in Wichita, Kansas
this year, a couple divorced in fighting over the fate of
Asher Nathanal Grisham's three-week-old (and already
newsworthy) penis: "Rodney Grisham believes circumcision is sexual assault. His wife argued that not circum-
cising their son violated her religious beliefs." She
belongs to the First Pentecostal Church, where "the pastor considers circumcision an important part of Judaic
Christian heritage."

What would either side make of the *Giba'at ha-Ghurlut*,
the "Hill of the Foreskins," as it rose at Joshua's bidding,
there upon *Gilgil*, under the eye of the Lord? "Forty years'
worth of foreskins," Edwardes calls it: "two tons' weight."
Two tons. As if a single knucklebone, or just one severed,
verdigris'd toe, as it drowses its sour eternity away in a silver reliquary, isn't amazing enough. *Two tons.* I wonder if
even Eliza's able fancy could accommodate the vision of

this diaspora of foreskins or the vision of, one day (when the Messiah comes?), their great repatriation.

Is it the womb? Is it the unitary speck that held the whole space-time continuum in utero? The nipple? The Garden? The round snug of the caves? What *is* this proto-loss so grand and deeply historied inside us that it causes us to cringe at any secondary loss that even *vaguely* seems mnemonic of it? *Where's that damn sock!*

In an early movie version of *Moby-Dick,* an exhausted and yet victorious Ahab safely commandeers his Pequod home to its New England shore: a laughable restructuring, except that it indeed speaks to our need for a circular closure.

⌒

She *wasn't* Mrs. Virgin Olive Oil.

She had her needs.

"Here. . . . No, *here.* . . . Yesssss."

They'd met at an Amity General picnic. Shelley was thirty-six and passable for ten years younger. Vern was also passable for twenty-six. He was, however, nineteen. He had the whole summer free, before college. Heartburn Vern, they called him, how could they not?—the son of Heartache Jake. That made it sweeter, sicker, extra low and extra heightened: the son of one of Randolph's medical colleagues. He had large, unknowing hands she loved to educate, and a large, vein-scraggled tuber of a prick. In addition, he hummed to himself, a *sotto voce* little-lost-boy's puff-up-my-bravery hum: she finally had a son, she finally had—despite, because of, Randolph's frequent absences—a lover. How could she *not?*

"Doll, you deserve it," said Giselle and made a lascivious show of unnecessarily slowly working her maraschino cherry off its stem.

But that wasn't it. She didn't *deserve* it. No, it was more as if her home life had become so tight around her, *so* constricting, she grew faint, saw stars, and came to—on occasion—in a different self, with this most different person nibbling sloppily over her naked flank. It felt as if she were *squeezed* out of a world where this was taboo and into a world where . . . well, where it was natural to love this way. Another bifurcated life.

To that extent, she shrugged off any blame. She was here, she was straddling Vern and then driving home to fix dinner, and if this was the result of a set of prerequisite conditions . . . it was Randolph who had engineered the conditions. It was almost as if he'd planned it this way for eighteen years—she'd married at eighteen—in expectation of the sack race on July Fourth when that goatee'd boy with the arms of a man would walk up with the park sun on his nape-hairs like a bristled incandescence and ask her looking straight in her eyes to be his partner. "And hell, even *nuns* get to feel they have a kind of husband every now and then," she once said to Giselle. "Who looks pretty buff in a loincloth," Giselle said.

Anyway, that was Shelley's necessary construct. It was different, as you'd guess, for Eliza.

"It was my sophomore year in college when they got the divorce. I told you: they both moved out, I sort of inherited the house. I took a year off from my studies, and just lived there. I'd *always* lived there, but now it was mine: I was a grown-up.

"And my mother took to visiting me . . . talking. Talking *everything.* I think I'd stopped being her daughter. I was more like Giselle—a friend, or a sister. And one night—we were, you know, merely gossiping men-this, men-that—she told me about her affair with this Vern. She just blurted it out like the most delicious confession you could imagine."

This is drink six, and Eliza lifts it overhead—it glimmers in the bar light—like a ditsy Statue of Liberty: it pleases the eye, both winsome and epic.

"I know what you're thinking, everyone thinks it: 'Good for her!' The poor mistreated wife. Well, maybe.

"But this was VERN, man. First off, he was a senior in my high school when I was a freshman—do we say 'freshperson' now?"

"*You* said 'But this was VERN, man.' You didn't say 'VERN, person.'"

"Right. Well anyway, I went to *high school* with him, and this guy winds up *porking my mother.*"

"I think the subtlety's lost on me, really."

"Porking. I said fuckingscrewinglayingporking MY MOTHER. Vern!—this ooh-I'm-so-cool crypto-Beatnik-wannabe who skims through *On the Road* one day and has his daddy finagle him a vanity plate for his Volvo that says CAROUAC. El dorko—trust me." [She pauses a moment.] "Not that I'd want to deny my mother or anyone their own strange tastes in matters of the pudendum.

"But it was the time parameters, finally, that freaked me out—that disappointed me.

"Sure, my father had cheated on her. But the Summer of Vern was a year *before* she'd come across the appointment books.

"She took up with Vern *not* as a wife betrayed, but as

a wife who simply didn't receive enough of her husband's attention.

"Sorry, I just couldn't help what I felt: I saw it as a weakness in her."

ꙿ

"We're all weak in *some* way, Eliza."

"Oh, I know." She lets out a basketball of a sigh, and then a chain of pool-ball hiccups. "Look at me, for instance." Laughs. "See? *Me, me, me:* is that a weakness, or what! I know, I know, I'm wussing on about the precious *moi*—and somebody somewhere else has Ebola. Somebody's getting a fist in her face." She mashes her fist at her nose in demonstration. "*Someone's* a paraplegic!"

"You want 'loss,' eh? [I say that in a spooky quaver; I'll tell you why.] Two days ago I got a snail-mail letter from Kendall—from my Austin, Texas life, way back. I hadn't heard from her in . . . oh, a decade. Then—kapow, this really long sweet letter of catch-up."

"Was she a girlfriend?"

"No. But a *good* friend. Now she's married, and. . . ."

I summarize this part of it: *Terryn, now fourteen months, despite being a truly great baby or perhaps because of it, was born missing the roof of her mouth. And I bet you didn't realize this, but the roof of your mouth is extremely important. It's critical for things like eating and talking, even breathing. Terryn cleverly learned how to eat using a special bottle despite the dire warnings of doctors about the need for all kinds of horrible things like tracheotomies and g-tubes (a tube straight into your stomach) and ear tubes. We managed to get her home, intact, at three weeks. Many of our friends and even the nurses at the hospital told us how lucky Terryn was to have such good parents*

*who can care for her so well. My thought to this was, of course,
if she was so fuckin' lucky, she would have been born with a
palate.*

"Oh my God."

"Not that we don't each of us have the right to be-
moan our hair loss or our cellulite. But, still . . . this isn't
even 'loss.' You can only lose something you once had.
This is a pure clean absolute Zero. Her stem cells screwed
up, right at the baseline. This is a newborn baby trying to
scream at the world with nothing but Nothing."

"Well, that shows me."

"Not that I want to lecture you or anything."

"Right. Professor Hair Loss."

⌒

The least-known of all Jack London's books, *The Star
Rover,* is a novel in the form of a soliloquy by "a prison in-
corrigible," articulate and resourceful death-row inmate
Darrell Standing. The scene is San Quentin (and later,
Folsom) in the first years of the century (the novel appeared in 1915). Standing is educated, and resolute, and
so becomes a special target for the venom of a sadistic
warden: "Standing, you *are* a wonder. You've got an iron
will, but I'll break it as sure as God made little apples."
One result: "At the present moment half a thousand
scars mark my body."

The chosen instrument of this warden's signature torture is a cunningly fashioned length of eyeleted canvas
called "the jacket." Into this, the prisoner-victim is laced
excruciatingly painfully. "My heart began to thump and
my lungs seemed unable to draw sufficient air for my
blood. I began to cry out, to yell, to scream, to howl, in a

very madness of dying. The trouble was the pain that had arisen in my heart. It was a sharp, definite pain, similar to that of pleurisy, except that it stabbed hotly through the heart itself." This was Standing's first time in the jacket: one half-hour's worth. He'll later hear of a man who's been inside the jacket (and not yet out) for fifty hours. Sometimes the warden and friends look on, with the pleasure of craftsmen proud in their labor. Standing will sometimes be in the jacket for *days.*

But Standing is a convict with astounding interior wells from which to draw. He learns to will what Leslie Fiedler calls, in the introduction to one edition, "the temporary cessation of bodily activity and a consequent liberation of the immortal spirit." Standing's effluvial self is freed: squeezed, tormentedly squeezed, from its physical housement. At the first, this projection remains unbodied: "I trod interstellar space. [And so the book's title; in Great Britain, it was issued as *The Jacket.*] In my hand I carried a long glass wand. It was borne in upon me that with the tip of this wand I must touch each star in passing. I, Darrell Standing . . . walked among the stars and tapped them with a wand of glass."[33]

Later, and really more interestingly, this free-flung spirit travels along a backward path through time, reentering bodies of its earlier lives. "I have worn the iron collar of the serf about my neck in cold climes; and I have loved princesses of royal houses in the tropic-warmed and sun-scented night. . . . I have been sea-cunie and bravo, scholar and recluse; yes, and I have led shouting rabbles down the wheel-worn, chariot-rutted paves of ancient and forgotten cities . . . and I have striven on forgotten battle-fields of the elder days." I summarize Standing's summary: there's *much* of this pneumatic reminiscence.

"Fictive reminiscence," I ought to say; but London's inspiration was a series of accounts in the popular press about (and, later, his own series of private interviews with) convicted felon Ed Morrell. The claim is: Morrell did, he "actually" did, experience the extra-corpus sauntering that London attributes to Standing. Arthur Conan Doyle (already oddly credulous of automatic writing, garden fairies, and ectoplasmic coils of ooze from mediums' ears and noses) also met with Morrell (a "clean-cut, deadly-earnest man") and he recounts it in *Our American Adventure* (1923).

Morrell, on his spectral jaunts: "Yes, sir, I dictated them to Jack with a stenographer taking every word. I did 10,000 words at a stretch once. It was all branded in my brain. I was like a man possessed. When I got waving a stick, Jack cried 'Stop! You put fear into me!'"

Doyle asks him, "What were these visions you saw?"

"'They were bits out of my own previous lives.'"

"How do you know they were not bits out of your readings?"

"'You've read them, have you not?'"

"Yes."

"'Well, how could they be things I had read when I was only a boy that knew nothing and had read nothing when I was jailed?'"

Doyle turns then to us and says, testimonially and sure, "This was true."

⌒

One semester I assigned *The Star Rover,* not because it's a splendid book—it isn't top-shelf writing—but because I hoped its story would appeal to my roomful of blue-collar Wichita, Kansas undergraduates: lawn boys, car hops, single mothers, part-time escorts, military retirees . . . each one of them with a need to escape from *some* box of unbearable confinement.[34]

Then there was Eliza, heir to relative privilege (for I teach at a school where a surgeon-father's salary and two previous years at Harvard count as a gorgeously regal privilege) . . . but on too many days she evidenced the pinched-in look of the rest. This was the semester I first met her. Her parents had been divorced; she was the house's only (and lonely: Jay was still in the future) occupant for a year; now, an occasional course at the local university. I didn't know this history then; or that in her freshman year at Harvard she'd already earned a foot-noted attribution in a scholarly astronomy paper. What I *did* know? . . . she was smart, she was funny, she bore this in her glumness in the way that tight black crepe still bears the light of a room on its surface.

They were keeping a journal of "readings responses." I found out who her father was:

"I have this crazy fantasy after reading Jack London. It has to do with a person's spirit (the 'soul'?) forced out of that person, as it is with Darrell Standing. Because for all of my life I've been around professionals who re-move, you name it, kidneys, colons, uteruses. Isn't that what Standing does? To keep on living, he needs to re-move his soul.

"And it merges with other bodies! Living, vibrant bodies! In my fantasy it can happen that way with wisdom teeth or ovaries, too. They fly through the air, and they live again in the gums of ancient Rome, in the groins of colonial Roanoke. It's crazy, so please forgive me, but I see it most with mastectomies. Individual hooters, hooters, hooters, swirling up into the air like a witches' Sabbath! And then they home on in to their respective kinship bosoms in past lives. Look!—one heads for Cleopatra's chest, one goes for Sojourner Truth's, Marie Antoinette's. . . . "Oh well, that's my readings report."

⌒

We like this bar, its mix. There are bikers wearing more leather than any single steer could ever provide; "just" housewives; sharp investment sharks; a few worn-flannel factory-late-shift men; occasionally, some hotshots from the pseudo-gang that likes to think it's tough; the guys we call "the loners with boners"; the do-si-doers; the lesbian bowlers (if it's tournament night); the "college crowd." It's loud, but never *too*. In back, a lanky fellow garbed all in black is eyeing down the length of his pool stick: focused on the ivory white of a cue ball with the intensity of Ahab aiming a harpoon at the ineluctable whiteness of his whale.

Here's how tonight came about.

Two nights ago—the night of the day I received Kendall's letter—I woke up from my own . . . let's use Eliza's language, why not . . . "crazy fantasy." It reminded me of (or was influenced by?) her own, from her journal a decade ago. And that was nudge enough for me to phone her up the next afternoon: "Yo, let's have a drink."

"Okay. *I* was going to call *you.* I have something to tell you, and something to ask you. Let's have" [*thinking*] "seven drinks."

The dream I'd had: I was soaring in space, from star to star, with a glass wand. I was lighter than air. I was faster than light.

But then . . . I was falling. Gravity changed, and I fell. I fell past stars, I fell *through* stars, I fell through a face the size of a firemen's net or a circus trampoline—and then through another, and then another . . . I fell through atoms, I fell through nothing, I fell through *less* than nothing, I was falling unstoppably into the space where Terryn's palate should have been but it wasn't, into that awful nothing-black . . . and out of it, riding to meet me, came a chalky equestrian skeleton-ghost, the one from Albert Pinkham Ryder's *Death on a Pale Horse,* and it wailed "You want loss, eh? You want loss, eh?" as if *it* knew, before *I* could, that I'd be quoting it—me, to my friend Eliza tonight, while somewhere some man's job is counting the stars and some star's job is counting the limited days of humankind's lives.

◡

A deep—approaching ebony—violet: this is the most appealing for a woman's mouth; and so the geisha finishes the contents of her small round porcelain lip-paints box, applying its color thickly with the puff-end of her brush and, with the point-end, silhouetting a petal-like shapeliness as finely as she can. She puckers briefly for her mirror and is satisfied: this new mouth floats intensely, like a berry in cream, against the even white matte that she's painted over the rest of her face, the gesso of a canvas. So

the lips, and the ink-bead eyes, and their accentuating
brows, become . . . not "sexy" quite, but "sexy" as implied through the lines of a sensitive abstract design.

The same care in selecting her obi—one of banded
jade and maroon? Or dragonfire orange? Either one will
set impressively along her char gray robe. And now a
final review of the sculpture she's made of her gluily
oiled hair—its central knot, its upswept side wings, and
the cantilevered tortoiseshell projections. Then arraying
her hand fan—just *so;* it will artfully speak of many kinds
of promise. Tonight, before her wealthy lover undoes the
pair-of-swans pearl clasp, the servant will kneel with tea
(and then depart, for the geisha herself will pour it into
the delicate eggshell cups), and then the two of them will
vibrantly discuss the new kabuki play, how achingly at-
tenuated over the course of long-drawn singsong notes
are some of the actors' gestures!—this, because she's not
a shop-whore, but a specialist whose taste and worldly
culture . . . whose refinement . . . whose accomplish-
ment in music and in letters . . . is, quite likely, something else (beyond her esoteric knowledge of "the arts of
love") that she *can,* while his wife cannot, provide a man
of status. Because it's 1800. Because it's the Yoshiwara
district of Edo, Japan—a part of that country's *ukiyo.*

—Which we call in English "floating world": "a place,"
Olivier Bernier says, "where the usual rules no longer applied." Think of it!—as if, let's say, a bud of Earth should
grow, pinch off, and be its own small satellite where gravity no longer counts as law.[35] Bernier: ". . . the quarters,
in all the larger cities, where brothels, theaters, teahouses,
and public baths were clustered. Every sort of entertainment could be found there, from classical theater and

music to cheap shop prostitutes, from an elaborate tea ritual and the attention of beautiful and highly educated
geishas to the most unchained orgies. These floating
worlds served an essential purpose: they were the one
place where men could escape the duties and obligations
of family and function." Right: another bifurcated life.

Is this a kindred species of what Dickens felt?—
deeply inhaling the frank sweat-musk of Ellen (Nelly)
Ternan's skin, there in the house he kept for her in
Houghton Place . . . and later the cottage in Slough . . .
and later "a substantial house" called Windsor Lodge
in Peckham . . . these were paid for by a "Mr. Charles
Trigham" or sometimes a "Mr. Thomas Trigham" . . .
or "Thomas Turnham" or "Frances Turnham" . . .
money funneled, hush-hush, through the "N Trust," as
he chose to call it . . . floating . . . she was eighteen, with
the springiness and sauce of what she was: a brainy, hun-
gry young woman, used to the ways, the backstage ways,
of an actress since age three . . . afloat . . . the two of
them . . . his wife renounced . . . the marriage was "insufferable," "a loveless chore," ten children (and that
great leech called "the public" with its vitiating adora-
tion) . . . here, however, Ellen, "Nelly," "N," "The
Riddle" . . . oh the scent of her arched underarms . . . a
sweet and secret drifting . . . "his relationship with her
forced him to become an escape artist, and it's because
of her that the last thirteen years of his life are filled
with periods in which they both seem to disappear."

And it was necessary, this sub-rosa imbroglio; or he
thought that it was. "He had created a role for himself
that was a terrible burden. He was the bard of the

hearth, so he couldn't suddenly cast off that role and appear publicly as the louche bohemian with a mistress. For
him, the public was one entity; and his relationship with
it was as intense as his relationship with a woman. His
friend Wilkie Collins could keep a mistress because he
had no status to maintain. But Dickens had created a
unique position for himself. His reputation became like
a medieval contraption of torture that encaged him"
(Phyllis Rose, Victorian scholar).

Necessary, yes—this furtive domain of aliases and en-
cryptions. But on *some* other level, surely, for an actress
and a fiction wiz . . . *desirable* as well? Telegrams were
sent in code. Railway routes of Daedalusian intricacy
were plotted. Trusted go-betweens were trusted with
part-truths and used for transport of his messages, trifles,
rents. An annual bonfire carried every one of Dickens's
personal letters out of this world. In the winter of 1868,
while in New York, he lost his leather pocket diary: this,
at least, we have, a scribbled-up exemplum of the subterfuge. "In his biography of Dickens, Peter Ackroyd
cites January 7, 1867, an ordinary day, as an example:
'The diary reads: *At G.H. All go. To Sl at 2.*' which, trans-
lated, means 'he was at Gad's Hill Place, that the Christmas party finally disassembled, and that he went on to
Slough, no doubt to his own "secret" cottage there before
visiting the Ternans' just a short walk away.'" A covert
record I suspect would crack one very slyly understanding smile from Columbus's stalwart mien.[36]

On the whole, it was all a successfully managed un-
dercover campaign. It wasn't until the 1930s that their
relationship started to enter public knowledge, more

than one-and-a-half dividing decades from her death, and over seventy years from his. (The pocket diary wasn't deciphered until the late 1950s.)

And Nelly, his accomplice-in-vanishing . . . what did *she* feel over those thirteen years of hideaway intimacy? And what, for that matter, slinked or soared, acquiesced or triumphed, on the back stairs in the mind of one Vern Nillson as he drove up to the door-of-the-day at Motel This or That and tapped a prearranged tune below its foggy peephole, waiting for Shelley to answer and whisk him inside, and rev up the engines that took them off the Earth to a moon of population two that floated the heavens?

What expression is in the wash bowl, late the following, lazy morning, as our geisha's slurred remaining slips of makeup swirl in the water, and seem—for just a nanotick of time—to reform into a face? Contentment? Weariness? Professional pride? The endless possibilities are lost in a runnel of water in the garden, and a single solid cherry-blossom petal on its surface only mocks attempts at questioning.

Nelly's thoughts and motives are, if anything, less apparent to us than are her lover's.[37] Some conclude she was (along with her ambitious actress-mother) a conniver and a calculating puppeteer of the genius novelist's heartstrings. (Certainly she became what we can justly deem a willing "beneficiary" of what we can in conscience call a greater "ease" than she . . . one of three sisters in a by-then fatherless family, and by all accounts the least theatrically talented of the three . . . could have expected out of life before that evening in July of 1857, in Manchester, when, in a benefit performance of the melodrama he wrote in collaboration with Wilkie Collins,

The Frozen Deep, the hero—Richard-Wardour-played-by-Dickens—died onstage in the arms of one of the actresses he'd hired on the advice of a friend, and according to Dickens, "Her tears fell down my face, down my beard . . . down my ragged dress—poured all over me; like rain," and as Richard Wardour the fiction perished, Charles Dickens the actor was smote.) Of course, an equal number of diagnosticians claim she was a powerless naïf, swept up by the dynamo force and celebrity of this man to do his bidding.

It was no doubt a more inblended coloration than the pristinemost of arguments on either side account for. She remains for us mercurial, and of the few things that we know for a fact, I offer two.

First: six years after Dickens's death, Ellen Ternan—then *thirty*-six—married the Reverend George Wharton Robinson—then twenty-eight—and gave her official age as *twenty*-six, which evidently she could pass for. In 1881, when she was forty-two, she offered the census bureau an age of twenty-eight.[38] In a life of probity (Epstein: "She sent her children to strict boarding schools, where they received conventional educations. Socially and politically conservative, she would never have seen herself as a feminist heroine. Indeed, in 1911 she joined the Anti-Suffrage League"), she still was a cupboard locked around secrets.[39]

And: well into this second existence, after she and her husband started the private boys school, after Geoffrey and Gladys were born . . . she still raised money for worthwhile causes by giving public readings from the works of the famous nineteenth-century author, Charles Dickens.

I think it's possible she felt toward him what Dickens's only outspoken child, the spunky Kate, so obviously did. As Miriam Margolyes puts it, "Kate once said 'My father is a very wicked man,' yet she loved him dearly. That's the paradox of Dickens."

"Albert," Eliza says, "don't get the wrong impression. Randolph Phillips *is* a great man, I'm convinced of that. Let me explain it. . . ."

‿

Her name is . . . let's say it's Leora Goetz. He's told her such frightening things!—it makes the deepest bones inside of her wilt like a marzipan in the heat. He's told her the knife will go in: here, and here: he touched her in those places. And he softly said: this will be removed; and this?—this will be forever missing, this will be gone like the snout of the Sphinx, like the arms of the Venus de Milo no matter how beautiful they were, no matter how many men would have shivered to think of their nearness, their surroundingness . . . they're gone. He said these things, her sister was in the room as well, to give her courage, and so her sister also heard and wept her courage into her upheld hands. Such frightening things. And yet he said them with a gentleness . . . she thinks about that, even now with the knife on her calendar only a week away, she calls that gentleness to mind . . . a manly gentleness is how she'd have to phrase it . . . and it makes her glad to have been there, makes her privileged to be its recipient. It hurt him to have to say those frightening things, she can tell. And yet he willed to take that hurt upon himself, for her. It brought them closer, she can tell. She knows; he touched her in those places: here, and here. She strokes those places with her fingertips, those places that are still here, that are here and here; she thinks of him. Her fingers travel over a hill, a beautiful hill, a hill of her. She thinks of him. He's standing in the sunlight, and he's calling to her. Calling—and she's following him up a beautiful hill that's here in the sunlight, near to her heart; following him up a beautiful hill, following him up a beautiful hill.

⌒

"The better it was with Jay, the more I could readily like my father . . . I don't know, it must have been those good times gave me a base of support, from which I could feel empathy . . . *something* like that. And then, too, 'better times with Jay' would always coincide, were *one,* with the best of my astronomical studies. I could see the separate parts of the universe interlinking, making, or anyway *trying* to make, a whole; and then I'd turn and see my father's life, which had come to represent . . . how should I put it? . . . disunity. Mother, too: she'd visit sometimes, I'd feel as if I were talking to a shape composed of little shifting kaleidoscope pieces. Finally I asked her not to come by. *Her* house!—and still I'd forbid her to visit. I was a shit. But I was *at war*—like some dopey comic book, with the people of the planet Harmony striving against an evil planet whose battle motto was: Shatter and Slice.

"But when everything soured . . . with Jay and me. . . . Have I told you before about the night on the casino boat?"

"I don't think so . . . no."

"Okay, let's have a last drink, and I will. It's there that I started to reconcile myself with my father." She gets very quiet: pool-ball clack from the back room is like firecrackers thrown on our table. Quiet, introspective. "It's a shame I never had the chance to reconcile with Mother."

"Did they *ever* find the driver of the other car?"

"Nope. One dead Shelley, and nobody else." Her hand makes a speed-away motion. "*Voom!* Her funeral was the last time I saw Jay. So that was two good-byes."

She's quiet again, and then, as if to rouse herself out of something so Eliza-unlikely as quietude, she says, "Whoooa, but the Ran-man is as spicy as ever. Seen him lately?"

"No, I have no reason to."

"He still looks *amazing* at fifty-three. . . ."

"Uh—I'm fifty-three."

"Well no offense, but the Ran-man still has this fuck-ing *wheatfield* of hair on his head . . ."

"How nice."

". . . and still works out every day on the rowing machine. He placed first for his age group in a national competition."

"How wickedly droll of him."

"*Don't* be pissy. And he's still active in the leadership of the Surgeons' Oncology Board . . ."

"The SOB?"—which she *steamrollers* over . . .

". . . and still gets spotted squiring slinky, half-his-age honeybuns around town. Last week a husband threat-ened to shoot him."

"I'll drink to that."

"Did I ever tell you that you're. . . ."

"Calm down, you *shaid* you wanted sheven drinksh."

"Oh very very hilarioush."

⌣

Now this is cobbled together from that night's talk and several earlier conversations:

Jay *was* astronomy. Astronomy was Jay. (And they had matching T-shirts, STARS R US, a sure yuk at observatory parties. Once . . . a New Year's bash . . . one colleague made a mistimed joke on Eliza's own "heavenly body"—Jay was forcefully dragged off the dumbfuck's face by three of the other attendees. "I thought: WOW, THIS is what love is! And that night we screwed in his van in the observatory parking lot, with the stars of a new year burning all over us, burning like pins in our bodies.")

"My Russian bear," she called him publicly. (It's the way I was introduced to him: "Professor Goldbarth, meet my Russian bear," and it was easy to imagine that only a moment before he'd been shambling around on all-fours, up bipedally at her finger's snap. He was huge, and shaggy—the cliché way some people would think a wild Russian composer of classical music, a four-star chess player, would be shaggy—*à la* Rasputin.)

And he *was* Russian (like her choices of astronomy and Harvard, one more bright link in a chain attaching her surely to her matrix-figure, Cecilia Payne-Gaposchkin). Jay, which was really J., which was really Javanovich, which was *really* pronounced Yawahnowich, which was really something impossibly cyrillicish to our hopelessly mallspeak-deadened American ears. "And isn't he *perfect?*" she'd say, and, of course, it *was* an ideal match, if fitting the demands of someone's fetish is ideal: he was an émigré—a child genius cut off from the motherland; a fragment; a Soviet peg in ("and *don't* make your *double-entendre* face at this") an American hole. Eliza's job (*she* saw it that way; "I think poor Jay was blind to it all") was seamlessly splicing her vagabond into the onrushing reel of life in the States.

And he *was* a bear. His thick inflection shaded off finally at its nether end into a growl. He'd lift his chalk to add some X to an equation, and you'd have to say the gesture was a "swipe." He might have flipped that chalk, a second before, from its place in a school of live chalk sticks in a silvery mountain stream. Not that he wasn't gentle; he *was,* the way domesticated bears in children's stories are. Although he could unleash the beast to pummel some jerk at a party, for Eliza and her friends . . . the way to put it is he'd spent years with a chair and a whip, to tame this thing inside him. "My sweet werebear," she would purr—a purr she'd picked up from her mother. And you could sense that the bones inside this massive body hungered mightily to configure for her in ursine ways. "I'd salute him: 'Major Ursa'—get it? The sex was— well, he would hug me to him—a bear hug, right?—and then this astonishing animal energy shook him in its grip, and then it dominoed into me." At which, she added, "Is this embarrassing you?"

It wasn't: in part because the sex was just an appetizing tease. The *real* meal all along—the true connubial connection—was their sense that life had given them joint custodianship of the night sky. Stars as lonely as a single spat tooth rattling around in a cuspidor; others, thickly clustered like the blooms of a field on fire . . . all of them, every giant and dwarf of the whole zodiacal circus, theirs for inspection and tagging. What Mendel was, to his peas—but these were the constellations! "Can a person feel humbled *and* imperious simultaneously? *We* were. We were drunk on that astral fizz."[40]

—An unlikely comparison, given the arid, numbers-crunching nature of so much of what was required of them. But her needs, and her cosmotaxonomy passions, weren't yours or mine: she was in love, the sky was open as an oyster with a squillion-plus combusting pearls imploring to be indexed, and I do believe she was, for a while, gloriously tipsy on the sudden, seemly adhesion in what seemed, before, an existence of sawed-apart discards.

"When we did that Jack London novel for class . . . ?"

"Uh-huh. I looked at your reading report and I thought, 'With a mind so feisty and sicko, this person is going to wind up a personal friend.'" I make the gesture of *presto-voilà,* and work up a falsely modest blush at the pinpoint accuracy of my prognostication.

"It's my fascination with older authority figures. Look at C."

"That's going well, right?"

"Yup. No complaints in the C.-section."

"Do you ever. . . ."

"Look, let me tell this my way, in my order. I'm all about order."

"Okay—London."

"Yes. His protagonist, Standish, Stanford, whatever, he has a vision that he's striding among the stars with a glass wand, sort of taking inventory. And that was me! Only, in *my* head . . . I was floating around in a French maid's apron and glittery stiletto heels, wielding a canary yellow feather duster. A star, *flickflick.* A star, *flickflick.* And each one was more lusterful once I'd touched it."

"That's you, kid. Bringing serious weight to cheaply frivolous fields of study."

"Albert, *give me a break.* Before this, I've told you a hundred times, [and *that's* a fact] it seemed to me that life was always slow-motion exploding. Pieces, flying away from me. And now, at last—that film was running back-ward. All the cows were coming home! The milk-carton children! Lost keys, donated kidneys, curbside litter, stolen cars! The little strayed lambs! The remnant toes from an-cient Roman statues! Seceded states!

"It was going to be an entire unblemished ball of unity! See?"—and she makes a globe of her hands.[41]

∼

We come to believe, in reading Jacques Barzun on the subject of Montaigne's sensibility, that there *are* rare indi-viduals who can look at Earth from a mind's-eye version of satellite height, and see it as a spinning marble, aqua blue and pocketable: as something a person could hold between his thumb and forefinger, turning it slowly, con-sidering every point along its surface with equal acuity.

For a few months, when her love and the domain of the observatory mingled while at their respective peaks, Eliza had finally attained that kind of holistic vision. Everything mattered; everything fit; nothing wasn't ac-counted for in the parade march of Creation. It was heal-ing—and endorphin-pumping. "Does any balloonist," Melville asks, "does the outlook man in the moon, take a broader view of space? Much thus, one fancies, looks the universe from Milton's celestial battlements."

What Eliza had forged for herself through luck and assiduousness was a happily viable combination of Montaigne's views and essayist Sven Birkerts's belief in a "core self"—this is his term, in one of his luminous pieces: "yes, I believe there is such a thing," a (now choose *your* word, "immutable," "changeless," "cen-tral," "insoluble," "resolute," or, from Eliza's point of view, "dependably there") identity, the still eye of our stormy lives, the fount of our sincerest credos, home to whatever passes in us for the quiet calm and focus, an atom of [*fill in your name*] that won't decay and reimage itself at the siren call of immediacy.[42]

Birkerts contrasts this to "the protean self—fluid and mutating according to situation and need," "decentered," "a more distributed experience of identity," and he's deeply troubled by what he sees as the protean self's ascendancy: "Our necessary ways of living are changing with breathtaking velocity. Multitasking behavior, already a norm, will be taken in many quarters as a paradigm, a successful adaptation to the forces and stresses of later modernity. And our individual sense of being cut off from something vital will grow stronger."

Cut off—the metaphor-world of the Ran-man himself. But Eliza had found what Birkerts here calls "something vital," and she wasn't letting (*her* words now) "any goddam *army* of cutlery slice off this thing from my keeping."

As Birkerts's chosen image is the core, Montaigne's would be—if he elected to represent himself so—the perimeter; and it complements Birkerts's picture. Montaigne acknowledges that people aren't uniform from day to day, even event to event; no, we've been sired by the primal flux and suckled by amoebas . . . and we've therefore grown up many-sided, "mountainous" as Montaigne says.

Barzun: "So many biographers declare the subject of their book 'a bundle of contradictions': he or she was generous to strangers and public charities but stingy with the family. Contradiction! Not at all, *inconsistency;* a contradiction kills its opposite; inconsistencies exist side by side." Montaigne, Barzun contends, was a contemplatist with "the ability to see both sides of the mountain at once." His thinking encloses our facetedness as the ancient circle encloses the variegated surface of yin and yang.

Eliza's saving vision was a map inclusive of both the core and the shell; that is, a physics of stability—of a woman in place in a world that itself was in place in a comprehended cosmos—much the way Newtonian physics (all of those omniexplanatory laws and comforting synergies she trusted, in her first days as a high-school astronomer-neophyte) structured everything that might otherwise be chaos into a system of kempt recyclings.

We could say it this way: if *Moby-Dick* is a manual on slitting part from part—of ship from shore and leg from torso, sense from sanity and whale-skin from its underside city of muscle and vein; if in taking its census it finds a lively citizenry of stowaways, the shanghaied, the marooned; if it gives office to those sawbones crew whose shipboard titles easily betray their skill in specialty aspects of butchery (the mincer, the chopper, the grinderman); and if it lifts its huge postmortem segments of leviathan in front of us with a proprietary zest (the whale's mosque-dome of a skull; "his unhinged lower jaw"; the lattice staves and the scaffolding; "the miracle of his symmetrical tail" offered for our astonishment as if the flukes were fishy twins genetically fused at the hipline; and the penis—"the grandissimus," which is "longer than a Kentuckian is tall, nigh a foot in diameter at the base"—the great foreskin of which, on removal, is cut with armholes and worn as a lucky slicker by the mariner charged with rendering the blubber); and especially if this book remembers that sometimes sailors accidentally tithe from their own bodies ("toes are scarce among veteran blubber-room men") . . .

—both sides of the mountain at once—

. . . we must see, too, that the novel acts as a treatise (or let's say "manual" again, meant with an etymological literalness, since I'll quote soon from the chapter "A Squeeze of the Hand") on things becoming whole, becoming mended. (After all, from the point of view of the ocean, a ship going down is not a loss, but a returning.) At one point, Ishmael serves in the circle of men who stand about the tub of decanted, cooling, and (due to the cooling) somewhat lumps-ridden spermaceti. "It was our business to squeeze these lumps back into fluid . . . my fingers felt like eels, and began, as it were, to serpentize and spiralize."

Into this sweet, ultra-absorptive and all-equalizing cetacean honey, Ishmael's consciousness dives, dissolves. "As I bathed my hands among those soft, gentle globules of infiltrated tissues, woven almost within the hour . . . I felt divinely free from all ill-will, or petulance, or malice, of any sort whatsoever. I squeezed that sperm till I almost melted into it . . . and I found myself unwittingly squeezing my co-laborers' hands in it, mistaking their hands for the gentle globules. Oh! my dear fellow beings, . . . let us squeeze ourselves universally into the very milk and sperm of kindness. . . . In thoughts and visions of the night, I saw long rows of angels in paradise, each with his hands in a jar of spermaceti"—or maybe wafting along the infinite pearly corridors of the stars, and through those spiraled chambers, recognizing each star with a quick tap of a glass wand (or a feather duster), and looking back at the small blue ball of earth, and back in time, to the point where man and woman, people and beast, existed in the round of the caves as wholly as yolk in its white, before the myths of discontinuity start, before Babel fell—when language was One.

ᴗᴧ

In this embracive cognitive milieu, Eliza reinvigorated her earliest childhood fondness toward her father. (She could afford to, now that her world was so emotionally rosy.)

"Yeah yeah, blah blah, he was absent so much of the time. But—! When he *was* here, his time and his mind and his heart at once, that man was *on!*

"In the winter we'd sled, in fact we built our own sled from scratch: it had a turning wheel, side rails, a flag with my name stitched on it, the works! And after, we'd go to the Corner Cantina and get hot cocoas and talk. He *listened* to me, I was six and he listened as if I were a peer explaining some intricate new clamping technique. He listened the way you do—"

"Just what I've wanted to be. Your father figure."

"But, seriously. He accepted me on my terms. In summer we'd go for walks at night and count the fireflies. He—well, this is just all treacle to somebody else, I can tell. But trust me: he could give me an hour that satisfied me more than the stupid boring condescending entire days that other kids received.

"And Albert . . . he was a warrior. I mean that. He never self-dramatized that way, but I learned. From my mother, when they were still in love. By listening around: when company came, or at the beauty salon, or the grocery. Everyone knew it, the way you'd know if Wyatt Earp or maybe Hercules were your neighbor.

"Every day, he went into battle. He fought armies of cells. *Armies:* except the cities that they overran and ravaged were human bodies. Every day he faced that enemy. While the rest of the world was shopping for dinner or filing forms or tuning cars or teaching sonnets (no offense meant), he was walking into the stronghold of Death and staring into its face. *You bet* I thought him a hero.

"Every day, he held the hand of someone brushed by the wing of dying."

I've heard many renditions of this from Eliza. Once, I remember (but not the night I'm recounting here), I tried to gently suggest that, yes, a man could be an excellent companion for his six-year-old, yet still be dabbling in damaging tastes.

Eliza only said, "He reached his hands into Death itself, Albert.

"Look, every warrior gets to have a shield.

"Give him the right to his."

⌒

A woman retraces her steps: a small oasis of light, the dark, a small oasis of light . . . pacing; nervous; trying to think it through. Because she told him, her husband the crazy sonofabitch. She shouldn't have told him, but she did, what the hell, her older sister was dead now, Leora, her dearest, who ten years ago she accompanied to the clinic to give her support, and met the mesmerizing Doctor Randolph eye to eye—and, even in that fraught traumatic time, she thrilled to the presence of him, way down inside, where something like a whirligig spun in her blood when he spoke, and nothing "happened" then, she left with

Leora, she dreamed, she masturbated, but nothing, you know, "happened," but now it was ten years later, Leora was in the ground, no, up in heaven, wherever, and then she'd heard from a friend whose friend had a friend in the know, that Randolph was "available," and she was as attractive as ever, wasn't she? and her husband the dried-up-shit-on-a-stick, the crazy bastard, couldn't care less, so she phoned him, he was listed, she was brave, she invented a story, they met, and see?—he had a whirligig, too! she knew he would! and it "happened," at last. Only now . . . now what? She'd told the crazy bastard. What to do? She paces. Across the street, on the deck of a bar, a man and his former student are chatting, the world is alive with action and noise, action and weird connections, noise and dissonance, he'd held his fucking idiot gun in the air like he thought he was Jesse James and said I'll shoot that asshole dead, which was bullshit of course, or was it, who knew? you never could tell with a sick scumbag like that who she shouldn't have married if he was dying of plague and promised her Fort Knox. Now what? A small oasis of light, and now what? into the dark, and now? the light, and now? the dark, and pacing away with her problems until the bar deck is a winking mote of dust on a faraway planet with its own and very different noise and action and weird connections.

 —Sarah G., from the *other* appointment book.

༉

"My last great time with Jay was the casino boat . . . we'd been squabbling a lot, and it didn't help that I was starting about this time to doubt my dedication to astronomy. . . . Anyhoo, we wanted to 'get away.' We rented a room for two nights. It was wonderful!

 "The sex was great"—how could it *not* be, rocking in a

hammock in their luxury berth and sensing the surrounding libidinous licking of the river?—"and the food, which I heartily recommend, and I even gambled a bit, not for the riskiness, but just to be in the company of those other coolly well-dressed nightlife people, they seemed so removed from standard, limiting middle-class mores: like, for all they showed of income tax or committee meetings or traffic jams, we might as well have been in a vacation yacht on one of the main canals of science-fictional Mars."

And *that* was the pleasure, really: not the sex or cuisine or roulette, or even the true illicit vices that the crew discreetly hinted could be safely sampled beyond an unmarked door to which they'd lead one for a generous "donation" . . . no, the actual pleasure was simply in being *away*—as if, in casting off from the gambling laws and liquor restrictions ashore, they headed into a completely separate domain of human experience, unconnected to the daily concerns of the rest of us by even a single spider thread.

"I'd stroll the deck alone . . . not lonely, just alone. As if the night sky were an amnion around me. It's a rightness I've never known before or since.[43]

"In the time of Herschel—the eighteenth century—they called the other galaxies 'island universes.' They really weren't sure *what* they were—those mysterious whorled enormities of light, on the opposite side of such absolute emptiness!—did they even dim and beam by the same laws of physics?—did they have the same God?

"And it seemed . . . as if I'd somehow become a denizen of one of those island universes, swaddled at the heart of layers of void and swarming suns, with my own loyalties and philosophies, unmoved by anything so remote as the petty responsibilities of Earth.

"I felt so *close* then to my father. I mean OBVIOUSLY—*mais oui, amigos*—OF COURSE, after everything weepy and ontological heaped on my father throughout a day, over years, he required his series of floating spheres to nest inside, above it all. I forgave his little meaningless philandering diversions. I *understood.* I mean, okay, so he wound up leading a somewhat . . . I'll say it this way . . . a compartmented life.

"But someone said to me once, a student of blues, 'If we couldn't compartment the breath, we wouldn't have the harmonica.' Think about it."

Huh?

But what I do think, when I look back at Eliza's words and try hard to consider Randolph Phillips's ultimate surgical dislocation—himself from the rules of the rest of the world—with labored empathy . . . what I think then is of Freddie Maguire, an antique toy collector in southern California. His specialty . . . "his love" would not be hyperbolic . . . is what we'd now call "boomer toys," from the fifties and sixties.

Freddie amassed a thousand or more—rare pieces, Japanese spaceships, classic critters from the Disney "middle era," vintage Barbies, G.I. Joes, an entire Neanderthal village of Fred and Wilma Flintstones. They were displayed on the shelves of a special room he'd added onto the house, devoted solely to these icons of his passion. A very joyous room, a church of colorful lithographed tin and yesterday's plastics.

There was just one door to the room, and this he'd

had designed to be only three feet tall. It locked: that kept the unwanted out (and except for his toddler daughter on special supervised occasions, that meant everyone). And the door . . . you see: he had to crawl in. He had to become a child again.

Drifting, in that closed-off space. *Ukiyo:* the floating world.

Another—willfully, pleasantly—bifurcated life.

"Of course, for all of this similarity," as I said to Eliza, "the consequences of toy collecting differ mighty immensely from those of adultery," and she had to agree.

⌒

"And then it all started to fall apart. You remember the party?"

"You and Jay left separately."

"Yup. And we never reunited. But the bickering, and the divorce . . . that was the public part. Inside me, it was paralleled by my lover's spat with astronomy. And I mean that pretty literally: I'd fallen in love at fourteen with astronomy—with a certain kind, a certain dream, of astronomy—and over the years it outgrew me. So astronomy and Eliza Phillips?—they got divorced. My leaving Jay was only an outward symbol of that."

We're done with drink number seven now, idly scribbling evanescent doodles on the tabletop with the wet from our glasses.

"Explain this some more."

She thinks for a beat, to arrange her next stretch of the narrative into a lucid exposition. Then she says, "When I was fourteen, and I read Cecilia Payne-Gaposchkin's autobiography—bam! I was smitten. I wanted to be a

clone of her. *She* dabbled in botany: so did I. *She* read
Shakespeare: I read Shakespeare.[44] *She* married a Russian astronomer: well, ditto. And as for the stars . . .
through her and what she meant, I could see how all of
that endlessness and all of that unknowableness out
there in the sky in fact was being ordered . . . domesticated . . . tagged . . . one element of the periodic table at
a time, one fiery asterisk after another . . . it was being
brought into a system of human meaning. That revela-
tion saved my adolescent sanity, I swear.

"So I was fourteen. The astronomy I loved was from a
moment in the century that *also* was around fourteen:
nineteen-fourteen. That's where it stopped, for me: with
counting and measuring and depicting these beautifully
rendered bouquets of orbits.

"But astronomy had been speeding away from that for
seven decades. I didn't know it, sitting there reading
about Copernicus and Caroline Herschel in Edison High
School study hall—I was only a kid. But I don't have to
tell *you,* Mr. Dabbler-in-the-History-of-Science, that astronomy was successfully wooed by physics, then by quantum physics. Suddenly it was all improbability theory,
anti-states, uncertainty studies, shrugging gradations of
relativism . . . I didn't need astronomy for that. I had my
parents for that. The more I pursued it at Harvard, the less
it served at assuaging my burble of wants.

"At fourteen I could plunk down an ephemeris on a
study-hall desk and obsessively read its pages of lists for
hours. At twenty-one, I was being told that 'really' there
wasn't a 'desk' [she makes those tiny claw-scrapes in the
air that mean quotation marks], just emptiness and various in-out, off-on fields of energy. Light was 'this,' but

also 'that.' The more you studied a result, the more it changed.

"And so there was the difference. There was the fist-in-the-face I couldn't dodge. Cecilia Payne-Gaposchkin was the real deal . . . seeking knowledge, ready to accept whatever weirdshit bogeyman shapes it assumed. Whatever cosmojuju. But me . . . ? I wanted an astronomy that would validate a preexisting schema. I was a failure."[45]

"*Heeey.* As I remember, you were the youngest Harvard astronomy major to have published a paper, ever."

"Sort of. I was the research assistant of five coauthors. Albert, that's a long time ago in career-years. And I'm happier now as a grade-school science teacher, really. It fits me better. Cecilia would have understood."

"Did Jay understand?"

"Oh, you know . . . yes, but not *truly* yes. It was one more thing to squabble about. I guess he saw it as a weakness—well, it was. As a betrayal. And *he* was the real deal, too. He forged ahead. He's done very important work. He doesn't know, but I follow it: there's an Internet site for his project group. String theory, expansion-coupling theory, maximal-helicon theory . . . things like normal thoughts gone inside-out.

"But I'm still content with a backyard telescope—C. got me one for my birthday last year.

"And Jay . . . became like a poster boy for a cause that was lost soon after the posters were printed. I abandoned him, I hated myself for abandoning him, and the certainties of what's essentially nineteenth-century scientific rationalism abandoned me. Those, I can tell you, were tough, tough times."

⌢

What she doesn't know I know—because I also know a former student of mine who now works EMS—is this: the pills that she used were half blue and half pink—as if to insist to the world that death is gender-inclusive. They were perfect yin-yang circles of he-death and she-death. Can a vial of pills the length of a baby's finger let in death the size of an adult casket? Yes, oh yes. Oh horribly yes. She fell to the curb, she hairline-split her skull. Can a swallow of medication orbit in the blood like a sputnik set to shoot out beams of death? Oh yes yes yes yes yes. She was there, in a runnel of reeking sidewalk god-knows-what when the ambulance arrived.[46] On phoned instructions from the hospital, they induced vomiting . . . "a pastel stew," as this person reported, "of little-girl pink and [perfect, for our poor astronomy dropout] sky-blue blue."

But all that's secret. (As you've probably guessed, these names I use are fictions. And this, what you're reading? . . . my public log; tweaked, as was Columbus's.)

When Shelley's old friend Giselle found out—the PTA diva herself—she arranged a meeting between Eliza and Carlota Santo, now the school district coordinator for education majors (and, in one of those tiny connection-synchronicities that make us shake our heads in wonder, the teacher who—her first year on the job at Edison's Junior High Auxiliary—had loaned Eliza that copy of Cecilia Payne-Gaposchkin's autobiography). Carlota was a sensible woman. And maybe, as Giselle claimed, it was time for Eliza to think about a sensible change in career track.

৶

"LAST CALL!"—that penetrating, foghorn voice. It needs to be: for some of us, a ball of fog *is* settled in our heads now. (For a couple of guys at the pool rack, it would seem to be at least as thickly packed as a bale of cotton.)

"But Eliza . . . on the casino boat . . . when you worked up an affinity toward your father's . . . um, 'compartmented' life. . . ."

"What?"

"Didn't it work up tender understanding toward your mother's affair?"

"It didn't. I don't know why. I'll tell you what does, however—too late, of course. Too late to make a peace between us." Suddenly: a softness overcomes her voice, as if it's a cloth washed one too many times. "I'm sorry: I blitzed out for a moment. I was saying . . . ? Oh right: I wish I *could* knock on the door of her grave and say 'Look, *I'm* the younger lover now of an older partner. These things happen. I understand. Forgive me.' Life is certainly convoluted, huh?"

"Well, it's heartening for *this* dirty old man to know that sometimes lesbians also rob the cradle."

"That's sweet of you; I'm afraid, though, I'm a teeny bit beyond cradle bait."

"Still, what's the gap between you and Carlota?"

Carlota Santo . . . C.

"Nine years. It may as well have been nine freakin' *centuries* when I was fourteen and she handed me—this old, *old* lady [giggles]—the Payne-Gaposchkin book. But when we remet over lunch with Giselle, after all that time . . . I mean, I'm thirty now. It's no big deal. When you realize for the first time that you're falling in same-sex love, with all of the dazzle, and all of the baggage . . . believe me: a few years here or there seem pretty trivial.

"But maybe there *is* one difference because of our ages—or maybe it's really only C.'s temperament, and she'd be this way if she were a bouncy nineteen, who can tell? In any case, as you know, she's *much* more private about it all than I'd ever be, except out of respect for her. No holding hands in public, no coy references of any kind: her closest colleagues don't even know that we live together. I guess," and then there's some more of that tabletop doodling-in-dampness, "you could say we keep a fake appointment book."

⌣

Every second of every day on the surface of water, the wedding of water and air takes place. Also every second: the wedding of air and air; of water, into water. The perfect connubial match of snow on snow, until there's only one snow. Of molecular bonding, the ordinary as well as the bodacious. In a *uni*-verse—a "one-holistic-turning-around"—there's room for them all. In Wells's *The War of the Worlds* the wedding of Earthly germ and Martian biosystem. (From the Martian point of view, of course, that pairing is unfortunate.)

Some interplanetary weddings are more festive than that, however. In a *Legion of Super-Heroes* issue from 1978—after real-time *decades* of simpering googoo eyes, bruised feelings, and shared adventures in the pursuit of outer-space hooligans—Lightning Lad and Saturn Girl exchange their thirtieth-century vows. We aren't told whether she takes his name or keeps her own or hyphenates (in which case, Mira Ardeen-Ranzz; and his would be Garth Ranzz-Ardeen) and we *definitely* aren't kept informed on the breeding potential of a couple that not only come from two separate planets, but out of two distinctly separate evolutions. Still, if the future can *ever* be read in the unsteady threads of the present, these two seem assured of their proper share of superheroic contentedness: maybe even of something so uncommon, we've almost let go of the word for it: bliss.

And similar couples, over the years, clump into immanence from the general pool of latent Legion possibilities: Ultra Boy and Phantom Girl, Brainiac 5 and Supergirl, Shrinking Violet and Duplicate Boy, Cosmic Boy and Night Girl, Mon-El and Shadow Lass, even Bouncing Boy and Duo Damsel, and Dream Girl (the one with the bare legs and the go-go boots) and Star Boy. Over vastnesses in which entire galaxies can sink from sight like pennies in the sea . . . these heed the call and are true to the difficult paths of pheromones, they sense the flame, they rise with the glorious itch, they toe the brink of the gulf in search of their completion.

There is no joining of hearts too out of bounds for *someone's*—somewhere—due consideration. I own a tattered, yellowing copy of the long-ago issue of *Superman's Pal Jimmy Olsen* with the cover tale "The Bride of Jungle Jimmy." There she is, beside him: a shrewish gorilla, complete with bridal veil. And in *Doom Patrol* #104 (1966), the fair Elasti-Girl wed Mento.

The original story of love—the matrix story, the one that was born in the first irradiant blossoming of the universe, the one that serves as source and model for each of our smaller quotidian loves—allows for every combination architected into the species, so long as protoplasm can make the appropriate shapes, so long as it works.

～

"So long as it works."

"It does! I think . . . well look, it's scary to say it out loud, but I think that I'm actually *happy* now. Me! I stopped obsessing nuttily over unity-versus-disunity junk, I stopped attempting to cramp my life into patterns that didn't fit it . . . I had to break the mold."[47]

"Big-time, my sapphic sweetie."

"Well, yeah! And C.'s a real honey to me . . . and you've tasted her cooking! She has a nursing certificate, too. Sometimes we play at . . . oh, never mind. Anyway, I *have* to tell you this: I've been heading to this all night. Last week we got married. . . ."

"WHAT."

"Got married. Not legally—as if I have to spell *that* out for you. But in a private ceremony that a Unitarian minister conducted in her office."

"Why wasn't I. . . ."

"Nobody was. Just the minister, C., and me, and about a thousand vanilla-scent candles."

"You could have. . . ."

"Wait. Waitwaitwait. Back to the cooking. This is *why* we decided, kablooey, to go get married. C. was preparing potato quiche. We grow them ourselves, in the garden. So she's out there, at night, and picks a couple, and comes back in and slices one. . . ."

Bingo. "YOU'RE WEARING IT RIGHT NOW." I point—"That's it, right?"

She squeals. "You saw! You knew!"

And I'm on my feet and yelling (a little sloshily by now), "Yo! Last call for everybody's on me! We're. . . ."

"Albert. No."

But Albert is warp-speed ZOOMING, Albert is High in Oratorial Mode now, ". . . celebrating my friend Eliza's [pause for MAXIMUM drama] marrrrriage!"

(Here, insert a Group Bar Cheer about the decibel level of your local air force flyover show on July Fourth. Also, some chummy boos.)

"Albert. If. C. Were. Here. She'd. Fucking. Smash. Your. Head. With. A. Twelve. Pint. Tankard. You. Darling. Well-Meaning. Shit."

"Well she isn't. And THIS," I point again, "is AMAZING."

"Oh, it has its precedents."

⌢

Yes. Traditionally it's a fish. In Pliny's accounts we find the legend of the wealthy tyrant (and obviously strategic schemer) Polycrates, who voluntarily threw a precious ring of his into the ocean, as a kind of inoculation against ill luck—he reasoned that this one loss would serve as his total apportioning of misfortune. But the next night in the royal palace, his chef ran from the kitchens with the astonishing news that the great fish for the regent's meal had been slit open, and . . . well, you can guess. "It is on show," Pliny says, "in the Temple of Concord, set in a gold horn." (*You* can guess, but think of the confusion of the lamentable chef: boxed on the ears and demoted, all for announcing this most wonderful news.)

And a lady—this is sixth-century Glasgow—came in

tears to Bishop (later Saint) Mungo: she had accidentally dropped her husband's gold ring into the River Clyde, and now was suspected of giving it to a lover. "The next morn," Mungo prayed and meditated, and asked that the first fish caught that day in the Clyde be brought to him for his inspection: "in its mouth was the ring."

And after another saintly bishop, Gerbold of Bayeux, was driven unjustly out of his palace by villagers frenzied with maliciously untrue rumors, he threw his signet ring into the sea and then retired to a hermitage. Time passed, and a local fisherman made an unexpected discovery in the slippery guts of his day's catch. Thus, "Gerbold was sent for and reinstalled in his palace at Bayeux, which he continued for years to sanctify, with first his living presence and with subsequently his holy bones."

Occasionally a fish's cousin serves. In 1996, an engagement ring that was dropped in the sea off the west coast of Sweden two years earlier reemerged in a mussel. Fisherman Peder Carlsson traced the owner, fire chief Bengt Wingstedt, "because his fiancée's name was engraved on the band."

Even without a fish or a fishly relative involved, such stories ask to be deemed worthy of our popping eyes. Ten years had passed from the day Karen Goode was tossed by friends into the sea "for a lark," and so lost the eighteen-carat gold ring given to her by her mother . . . when she was strolling along her local beach at Freshwater East, Pembroke, Dyfed, "after the tanker *Sea Empress* oil disaster," and, looking down, she saw . . . well, you can guess, you can hear not only her cry of startled—her almost unbelieving—delight, but also *(listen . . . sssh . . .)* the tiny *tk!* of return, as when a dislocated bone is set back into its socket again, only this is the body of world and time, and not a human body, yet even so, the sense of recompletion isn't less for the body's being more diffuse.

Just name an animal. Around Easter of 1993, the wife of Norwegian politician Asbjŏrn Nŏstmo, Evelyn, lost her wedding ring as the two of them pushed their car from a forest snowdrift. Three years later, "Asbjŏrn's hunting party bagged a bull moose nine miles from where the ring had been lost. On 20 October 1966, Evelyn Nŏstmo was busy cooking the entrails when her eye was caught by a golden gleam . . . ," etc. Or how about Barry Stroop of Xenia, Ohio, who was hoeing his carrot garden in July of 1991 "when he chanced upon a man's gold diamond ring," and remembered his friend Woody Lott had lost just such a ring—as it turned out, of course, this very ring—in 1985 on Lott's mother's farm. "Twice a year, Lott carted manure six miles to Stroop's carrot garden for fertilizer. He guessed that a cow had eaten the ring and passed it in a load of manure."[48]

As Saturn Girl and Lightning Lad are our bathetic versions of the Elder Gods of yore, and reenact—for our own small Ramada Inn and baconburger lives—the cosmic rituals of struggle and redemption, so these cycling rings (much loved by local news shows when they need a hit of "warm and fuzzy" to leaven the usual leaden fare of war-torn nations and scandal) are our own prize-in-the-cereal-box, our dangle-from-the-rearview-mirror, versions of what the scholar of comparative religion Mircea Eliade has called the Myth of Eternal Return, which—for contemporary us—evokes the vision of Osiris's hacked and scattered body (fourteen pieces) sought out and reunified by Isis; and Jesus' agonized boomerang travel into, and out of, death; and the carousel rounds of a year itself, dying, reigniting like the phoenix, dying, re-igniting, all the while bearing on its ever-turning plate the four-part burden of the seasons; and the great renewal-tail in the great all-hunger jaws of the Uroborous, the Universal Serpent that has no start and no end.

In this construction, Jonah *is* a "ring": he enters ("visits" is more accurate) the belly of the monster fish; he languishes within its stinking, peristaltic systems; and, miraculously, he's reborn from that salty gullet (aka vagina), giving a single human face to what we sometimes more abstractly term the "circle" of life. He reaches shore, and . . . *tk!*

And if we're not up to a stay in the fabled whale, if our carport days and barfly nights don't seem to be touched by other-level Presences either angelic or demonic . . . still, we have our tabloid tabbies and pooches that—after wandering over sometimes hundreds of miles of alien terrain, including mountains, rivers, and difficult whizzing grids of urban traffic—verifiably arrive back at the porches of their owners, who had always already "given [them] up for lost." And yet they aren't lost, they're *here,* to be a thumbed nose and a loud razz at the hobgoblin minions of Chaos and Disarray.[49]

My own favorite example these days (besides Eliza's potato) is from that letter Kendall sent to me. It's only two sentences, simply done—"Eventually we did discover a surgeon to repair Terryn's palate. He did a good job."—but it speaks to me with the power of the Gospels.

⌣

"Carlos." *Clink clink.*

"Carlos! Yesss!"

"To Carlos!"

"To Carlos: a lucky man!"—and the man I invented licketysplit as a cover story, a "cover groom," to help protect the privacy Carlota so dearly values, and which I, the "darling well-meaning shit," came hairsbreadth close to riddling with perilous peepholes.

Last call, i.e., for Eliza and myself: an unexpected drink eight.

"To Carlos! I wish I could be in his shoes!" And a gravelly voice from an unknown source in the pool room: "And then in the bride's pants." Much guffawing, in a rough, good-natured way.

"Aiy, Carlos! El rey del bueno suerte! Yeeeeehah!"

This Carlos guy gets more appreciation than my last three books of poetry combined, and the foghorn bartender adds some mystery exorbitancy to my credit card, and Eliza is sitting between a solid keg of a woman wearing a sleeveless HADES MOMMAS leather vest, and a sweet geek fellow who looks like he's a volunteer accountant for the Catholic parish outreach group, the three of them irruptively harmonizing on "Here Comes the Bride" and then (as, I can only guess, what's meant to be a sign of solidarity with Carlos's supposed hot-as-a-jalapeño Latino roots) "La Bamba," and this goes on for a long, long time, until the lights blink twice and the bartender growls and the crowd tilts homeward and out the door, and then Eliza and I are left around 3 A.M. on the closed-down street-front deck, a little worn, but hangin' in there.

"Well, time for us to traipse home, too, kiddo, even if in your mixed-up heart you really do lust to sleep with me."

"Hey, I love you, Albert. You know—like an older brother."

"Our little secret. I won't tell my wife."

"I won't tell my lesbian husband."

⌣

"And this is what I need to ask you"—we already both hold car keys in our hands—"what I tried to arrive at all night. A question . . ."[50]

I make my face go *yeah? and? so?*

". . . about whether I should even mention this to my father, there's just SO much laden history between us, and he carries SO much emotional freight of his own about these things. . . ."

"Getting married? You *know* he'd understand."

"No, not quite that. Not that. [*a pause*] The two of us took a honeymoon, only a couple of days of camping . . . and I thought I'd get a clearer sky than we normally see in the backyard . . . so we drove up north to the foothills . . . and relaxed, you know, and spent some quality lovemaking time," she takes a breath, and there's a painting of Albert Pinkham Ryder's, *The Flying Dutchman,* where the waters are so heavy that they must be described in the colors of land, slate gray and malachite green; and where they peak and break and become almost claws in the fulminant air above the sailors' lives, these waves are less like water and more like slabs of thick lead crystal shattering in raking, jagged tips . . . the books on Ryder use such words as "violent," "turmoil," "turbulence," "churning," and yet, of course, the paint itself, the what-we're-looking-at, is motionless and fits by definition into the boundaries of its canvas . . . it could be shrunk down just a little and it would fit behind the locked door of a sternum, it would fit—this dense, apocalyptic heaving—in a heart, and only a hint of its bitter moisture would appear in the eyes and gather there, a breath, a gurgled breath, and then she says, "I have a lump."

Notes

‿〷

When one tugs at a single thing in Nature,
he finds it hitched to the rest of the Universe.

—JOHN MUIR

1

"All my life I have had an awareness of other times and places. I have been aware of other persons in me.—Oh, and trust me, so have you, my reader" (the start of Jack London's *The Star Rover,* 1915).

2

"Dickens wrote *Nickleby* when he was twenty-six, and
the first half of the novel contains as many great characters as any normal novelist would expect to produce in a
lifetime" (playwright David Edgar, quoted in *The Friendly
Dickens*). An interesting sci-fi variant on that marvelous
Victorian mind occurs in a novel of Clifford D. Simak's.
Carter Horton, the hero, is conversing with Nicodemus,
a robot:

> "You mean you have a box of auxiliary brains
> that you just plug in!"
>
> "Not really brains," said Nicodemus. "They are
> called transmogs, although I'm not sure why. Some-
> one once told me the term was short for trans-
> mogrification. Is there such a word?"
>
> "I don't know," said Horton.
>
> "Well, anyhow," said Nicodemus, "I have a chef
> transmog and a physician transmog and a bio-
> chemist transmog—well, you get the idea."

3

This skill in nimble-fingered microfinessery takes many forms. In his studio on the island of Jersey off the British coast—that is, away from the obviating vibrations of city traffic—a man named William Wigan carves, from lilliputian material such as a grain of sugar or speck of sawdust—statuary that "can rest on a human hair with room to spare.

"Many would remain invisible to visitors without the aid of a 200-power magnifying glass. Wigan has learned to control his nervous system, blood-flow and breathing—sometimes holding his breath for three minutes. He cuts only in the 1½ seconds between heartbeats."

I'm looking right now at a photograph of Snow White and the seven dwarves—each, an independent figure in brightly colored Disneyesque costume; each, in a recognizable pose, and with personality crafted into its features. The eight are lined up, without crowding, without even touching at all, in the horizontal-positioned eye of a standard sewing needle.

4

Bravery should also be noted.

The English novelist Fanny Burney underwent—"endured" is the verb that Marilyn Yalom chooses—a mastectomy in October of 1811, after reoccuring pains had encouraged a visit "to Napoleon's famous army surgeon, Baron Larrey." Yalom: "Burney's description of the surgery itself remains one of the landmark moments in the literature. Her story is told with such lucidity that we marvel at the author's courage, both during the harrowing procedure and afterward, when she forced herself to relive it in writing."

Through a transparent cambric handkerchief placed on her face, the patient can see "the glitter of polished Steel" as it hovers like the sheen off vultures above her available body. She feels the doctor's finger tracing a line "from top to bottom, secondly a Cross, & thirdly a Circle," and only then understands exactly what this muteshow means: the entirety will need to be removed. After that: "the terrible cutting," the intimate touch of a knife against the underlying bone: in all, full twenty minutes of "utterly speechless torture" that was, as Yalom reminds us, "performed on a fully conscious woman whose sole anesthesia had been a glass of wine." She survived, and lived nearly thirty more years.

Her heirs—I mean by this her spiritual heirs—are staring at me, seated behind a banquet table in Frederic

Brenner's photograph from 1994, "Survivors": six mid-dle-aged mastectomized women (one doubly so), who are unashamedly naked from the waist up, very gently but determinedly looking straight into the camera, and saying something about their grief, and their overcoming of grief, and their toughened joy in being here at all, and what they know (that any dictionary never will) about the word "acceptance"—saying this in their loud qui-etude from behind a table that holds a bowl overspilling with voluptuous fruit and a bowl of the same dimensions that's empty. The women hold hands: they form a chain. All six are Jewish: thereby, the idea of "survivors" is al-lowed an extra texture. One of them wears a necklace decorated with three large pendants, taking our eyes to just the space at which her cleavage would normally start, as if in proud display of her asymmety. The surgical scar itself is artfully covered in a lithe, unscrolling tattoo.

This woman is Deena Metzger who in 1980, three years after her mastectomy, appeared as the nude in a now quite well-known photographic portrait. She stretches her arms to either side and lifts her face to the sun with a fierce, triumphant smile. Marilyn Yalom says: "a stun-ning, life-affirming gesture," reproduced for years on post-ers and calendars: *The Warrior.*

But "war" can't enter—even through so slant a means—this note without my mentioning the losses that Walt Whitman witnessed, serving as a comforter and cot-side confidant of soldiers wounded in the War Be-tween the States. "One man is shot by a shell, both in the arm and leg—both are amputated—there lie the rejected members . . . all mutilated, sickening, torn, gouged out."

One entry has us see a cart that's filled to *mounded* with the sawed-off arms and legs of these dispensable men—these warriors.

As part of his compassionate labor, Whitman often wound up writing letters to the families of the deceased. One, which I'll quote from here, contains what surely must be—through its context—one of the most ironic appearances of a surname in our language. "Dear Madam. No doubt you and Frank's friends have heard the sad fact of his death in hospital here, through his uncle, or the lady from Baltimore, who took his things. I will write you a few lines—as a casual friend who sat by his death-bed. Your son, corporal Frank H. Irwin, was wounded near fort Fisher, Virginia, March 25, 1865—the wound was in the left knee, pretty bad. He was sent up to Washington, was receiv'd in ward C, Armory-square hospital, March 28th—the wound became worse, and on the 4th of April the leg was amputated a little above the knee—the operation was performed by one of the best soldiers in the army, Dr. Bliss. . . ."

Imagine the freighted, cawing laughter of Fanny Burney at this.

5

I'm reminded of how, through literature, our everyday emotions are provided with their larger-than-lifesize correlatives.

This stripper, who could easily be behind you impatiently holding a quart of milk and a clutch of romaine at the supermarket, looking just like any other yawning midday shopper . . . she requires some character out of a novel to act in our lives as her lobbyist. (So do you, to her; me, to you.)

Charles Baxter, writing on *Moby-Dick,* refers to "the novel's central figure, a maniacal, wounded, self-dramatizing, and obsessive sea captain." Then, his astute insight: "His wound is larger than his missing leg—Ahab is all wound. Nothing that he says is adequate to the wound."

6

Not that there isn't, especially by now, a ready access to a wealth of more acknowledgable assistance. "It's the biggest disease on the cultural map, bigger than AIDS, cystic fibrosis, or spinal injury, bigger even than those more prolific killers of women—heart disease, lung cancer, and stroke. There are roughly hundreds of websites devoted to it, not to mention newsletters, support groups, a whole genre of first-person [survivor] books; even a glossy, upper-middle-brow, monthly magazine, *Mamm* . . . [and]—while AIDS goes begging and low-rent diseases like tuberculosis have no friends at all—[*this* has] a generous flow of corporate support . . . Revlon, Avon, Ford, Tiffany, Pier 1, Estée Lauder, Ralph Lauren, Lee Jeans, Saks Fifth Avenue, JCPenney, Boston Market, Wilson athletic gear—and I apologize to those I've omitted."

This, from Barbara Ehrenreich, whose essay follows its story from her own first diagnosis through the surgery and the recovery. She discovers "four distinct lines, or species" of relevant teddy bears (including Hope, who "wears a pink turban as if to conceal chemotherapy-induced baldness"). These "are only the tip, so to speak, of the cornucopia of pink-ribbon-themed products. You can dress in pink-beribboned sweatshirts, denim shirts, pajamas, lingerie, aprons, loungewear, shoelaces, and socks; accessorize with pink rhinestone brooches, angel pins, scarves, caps, earrings, and bracelets; brighten up your home with themed candles, stained-glass pink-ribbon candleholders, coffee mugs, pendants, wind chimes, and night-lights; and pay your bills with a separate line of Checks for the Cure. 'Awareness' beats secrecy and stigma of course, but I can't help noticing that the existential space in which a friend has earnestly advised me to 'confront [my] mortality' bears a striking resemblance to a mall."

There are all sorts of warriors. There are as many kinds as roses, halls of fame, or curries. There are those who pose for the calendars, with their sheared chests bared in the wild, insistent beauty of one who's lived though a harsh apprenticeship and now wears its scars like epaulettes of a victory.

But then there's also Barbara Ehrenreich, rogue warrior, whose indignation takes aim at not only the savaging nature of the disease (and "the current barbarous approaches to its treatment"); and at the duplicities of the very, *very* remunerative medical establishment that has built its spread of palaces around this disease ("routine screening mammography is, in the words of famous British surgeon Dr. Michael Baum, 'one of the greatest deceptions perpetrated on the women of the Western world'"); and at a corporate greed that links the manufacturers of carcinogenic pesticides with the funding sponsors of various "awareness programs" (quoting the Cancer Prevention Coalition on "a public relations invention by a major polluter which puts women in the position of being unwitting allies of the very people who make them sick"); *but also* at the "cult" of "brave fighters," the ranks of the pink, the attitude police, for whom "cheerfulness is more or less mandatory, dissent a kind of treason. . . . No, this is not my sisterhood."—That last, perhaps the most difficult statement offered in a regimen of gruelingly difficult statements. "I know this much right now for sure: I will not go into that last good night with a teddy bear tucked under my arm."

Although I believe a mass-marketed Bear-bara Ehrenreich teddy—its button eyes of penetrating transparency; its fur the color of real bear, not angel poo—would do us all a world of good.

∿

Of heroes . . . there are as many kinds as there are cable stations, or definitions of "good," or handed-down chili recipes. The One-Arm Bandits are softball players, all seventeen of whom (but three) "are missing an arm or part of an arm. Asked why he includes three able-bodied players on his team, Victor laughed: 'We don't discriminate.'"

The team has been inducted into the Baseball Hall of Fame Library. Their first game—against a "regular" team—they lost by nine runs. Their second, they won by twelve. "In their fifth season they were so good they won ten of their twelve games." "God didn't give us all the limbs we need, but maybe he gave us a little bit more heart."

I like the picture of them running the bases, sliding into home: these guys (and a woman, Trish) whose surfaces look incomplete, and yet whose play on the field produces—just as well as anyone's—the semiotics of closure.

7

George Eliot—that made-up thing, so the unremittingly analytic and deeply commodious mind of Marian Evans could wend its way through the world without such doo-dah as gender ("female writers," etc.) and moral laxity ("living in sin," etc.) deflecting its thinking's proper, published course. At first the device of a pseudonym was a convenience; and eventually, a second—and in some ways an equally potent and equally necessary—self.

What was it like?—to wake, and sit to tea, and see to the household ledger books, as Marian; and then to turn to face the writing desk, with the molecules of her turning, too (increasingly, as her mind turned), into more and more of George. Her final novel, the polished and intricate puzzle box *Daniel Deronda,* asks to be the study of one well-bred, highly proper Victorian gentleman whose identity as a Jew is only very slowly revealed to him. His "secret identity" we could say, hijacking the jargon of comic books. Superman himself was created by Siegel and Schuster, two street-scrappy teenage Jews in a time when the world was less than openhanded to their kind; it's no surprise to find their boyish daydreams tending to goyish aliases, disguises, and hidden, Golem-like heroics.

(The conflictedness of bearing two identities: in the 1930s, Hitler offered Fritz Lang, a Jew—and director of such film classics as *M* and *Siegfried* and *Metropolis*—the post of Director of Third Reich Cinema Industries. Carlos Clarens says, "The same night the offer was made, Lang crossed the border.")

8

A partial list of the Legion of Super-Heroes membership and their secret identities: Phantom Girl is Tinya Wazzo; Triplicate Girl is Luorno Durgo; Brainiac 5 is Querl Dox; Lightning Lad is Garth Ranzz; Invisible Kid is Lyle Norg; Shrinking Violet is Salu Digby; Cosmic Boy is Rokk Krinn; Chameleon Boy is Reep Daggle; Saturn Girl is Mira Ardeen; Colossal Boy is Gim Allon; and Sun Boy is Dirk Morgna. And the squinty, bookish Latin teacher who comes home loaded with papers, kicks her pinchy shoes off, sighs, and then removes her blouse and so unveils—were we there to see her naked shoulder— her resplendent BORN TO PHUQUE tattoo from an earlier life . . . an earlier her.

But what they get in the teachers lounge is a serious gaze and a curt, unvarying smile. Marian Evans, who knew a thing or two, says: "So much subtler is a human mind than the outside tissues which make a sort of blazonry or clock-face for it."

᠊ᢙ᠊

The sudden sense of being as halved as a bivalve overruns all of us sometimes. How could it not?—the tug-of-war between the neocortex and the brain stem is a signal condition of being human.

The narrator of John Banville's novel *The Newton Letter* retires to the countryside to complete a long-overdue book he's at work on; but everything there—the field life, the touch of the sun, the air's smell—is distractingly strange. "Even the pages of my manuscript, when I sat worriedly turning them over, had an unfamiliar look, as if they had been written, not by someone else, but by another version of myself."

⌒

Still, Lightning Lad demonstrates time and again how separate halves can be made into a single smoothly functioning dynamic. "My hands are like the positive and negative poles of a battery! Each time I clap them together, a super-lightning flash leaps forth!"—with which, on this occasion, he forms the electroskittery letters of "a gigantic sign . . . visible for a million miles in outer space," so warns the Nova Express that its fuel tank is leaking.

He could be quadrapolar, nonopolar, as many-wedged as a tangerine, but he carries those selves in the easy way a verb carries its conjugations.

9

In Richard Wilbur's "Poetry and Happiness," he explores the drive to compile lists: "A primitive desire to lay claim to as much of the world as possible through uttering the names of things, turns up in all reaches of literature heavy or light—to possess the whole world, and to praise it, or at least to feel it. We see this most plainly and perfectly in the Latin canticle *Benedicte, omnia opera domini.* The first verses of that familiar canticle are:

> O all ye Works of the Lord, bless ye the Lord:
>> praise him, and magnify him for ever.
> O ye Angels of the Lord, bless ye the Lord:
>> praise him, and magnify him for ever.
> O ye Heavens, bless ye the Lord:
>> praise him, and magnify him for ever.
> O ye Waters that be above the firmament, bless ye
>> the Lord:
>> praise him, and magnify him for ever.

I needn't go on to the close, because I am sure you all know the logic of what follows. All the works of the Lord are called upon in turn—the sun, moon, and stars, and winds and several weathers of the sky, the creatures of the earth and sea, and lastly mankind. There is nothing left out. It is a poem or song in which [and here Eliza, the empyrean's own bean-counter, comes especially to mind] heaven and earth are surrendered and captured."

ꙮ

One lushly extreme example: according to James Elkins, the *Dictionnaire mytho-hermétique* by Antoine-Joseph Pernety lists *over six hundred* synonyms for what's commonly called the Philosopher's Stone.

10

Some time later, I asked to see it. "I also have one for penises, if you're interested," she said helpfully. [Joke:] "You'll think it's longer than I will."

Here, a partial list of the secret (slang) identities of the mammaries: Apples. Avocados. Baby Havens. Bagpipes. Bags. The Balcony. Balloons. Balongas. Bazongas. Bazoombas. Beauts. Begonias. Berries. Bobbers. Boingers. Bongos. Bonkers. Boobies. Boobs. Boulders. Bouncers. Bowling Balls. Bra Bombs. Briskets. Bubbies. Bubbles. Buffers. Bumpers. Bushels. Butterboxes. Cachowngas. Cakes. Canteens. Casabas. Chalubas. Charleys. Charms. Cheechees. Cherries. Chestnuts. Chichibangas. Choozies. Chowchows. Coconuts. Creamjugs. Creampuffs. Cuddlers. Cupid's Kettledrums. Cushions. Dairies. Danglers. Dials. Diddies. Dingleberries. Dollies. Dribblers. Droopers. Dumplings. Eggplants. Equipment. Faucets. Feeders. Finger Food. First Breakfasts. Flight Deck. Flip-Flops. Fried Eggs. Front-and-Center. Fun Ones. Futons. Glands. Globes. Glories. Goodies. Goonas. Gourds. Gourmet plates. Grand Tetons. Grapefruits. Grippers. Handfuls. Handles. Hangers. Headlights. Hemispheres. The High Valley. Hill Country. Honeydew Melons. Hooters. Jellies. Jigglers. Jimjams. Jugs. Jujubes. Kahoonas. Knobs. Knockers. Kumquats. Lactaters. The Ledge. Lemons. Lollies. Love Bites. Love Bumps. Lovelies. Lunchables. Lungs. Malteds. Mamms. Mangoes. Maracas. Marshmallows. Melons. Mildreds. The Milk

Shop. The Milky Way. Mosquito Bites. Mounds. Muffins. Murphies. Nay-nays. Nibbles. Nice Pair. Nice-To-Meet-Yas. Nick-Nacks. Nubbies. Nuggets. Num-Nums. Nutrition Farms. Oranges. O Wows. A Pair. Pancakes. Panters. Paps. Parachutes. Peaches. Pellets. Pillows. The Playground. Plumpers. The Prow. Pumpers. Pup Tents. A Rack. Rib Cushions. Risers. Rock and Rollers. Rockets. Roundabouts. Sacks. Sensationals. A Set. Shock Absorbers. Shoulder Boulders. Silly Putty. Sippers. Slurpers. Sugar Cubes. Superdupers. Sweet Potatoes. Swingers. Tatas. Teacups. Terrificos. Tiptops. Tits. Tonsils. Tooralooras. Top Ones. Treasure. Treats. Tremblers. The Twins. The Two Bald Uncles. The Upper Deck. Volleyballs. Wallopies. Wap-Waps. Watermelons. Waterwings. Wellsprings. Whamjammers. Whappers. Willets. Wonderfuls. Woowoos. Yayas. Yummies. Zingers.

"Once in my father's waiting room, I heard one of his patients refer to herself—good-naturedly, not bitterly—as 'cyclops chest,' which I thought was fiendishly clever. And another woman once pointed and said 'the Lone Ranger.'

"Me, I only tried for terms I could imagine being *somehow* used in a context that was positive. So, like, 'hog jaws' didn't make my list—maybe that's a failure of imagination on my part." And Eliza's added two terms of her own which, ever since, I've often had occasion to remember. One: sunrises. The other: teardrops.

⌒

Japanese: *chichi.* Small, *non-chichi.* Planetoidal, *zo chichi.* Especially estimable, from a sexual point of view, *chichi kurushii.* Also *opai, mune, paiotsu.* For a man to come from the friction supplied by a lady's cleavage: *tanima no shi-rayuri,* or "white lily in the valley."

⌣

And "ornaments"—so true. In her poem "The Shower," Kimiko Hahn presents a woman of seemingly later age ("nursing was precious and erotic, both / and it is over") who thinks: "What to make of these / ornaments, these empty chambers / that sting with pleasure even as / the skin begins to loosen?"

⌣

In *Naked,* David Sedaris's second collection of comic memoir, there's a moment when the author describes a book of cheap porno he chances on in his childhood: "The first two times I read the book, I found myself aching with pleasure. The third time I came away shocked, not by the characters' behavior but by the innumerable typos.

"In the opening chapter the daughter is caught with her brother's *ceck* in her *pissy,* calling out '*Feck* me hard, *hardir.*' When on page thirty-three the son has sex with his mother, he leaves the woman's '*tots* glistening with *jasm.*'"

11

As in those intellectual confections, the *ficciones* of Jorge
Luis Borges, where we're tempted into trying to define
the point at which a map as large as a place, as detailed as
a place, then *is* the place; the same with a mirror and face;
the same with a book and its story; the same with the
ideal library's infinite holdings and the world.

12

Also see the metaphysically powerful three-lines-of-a-poem "The White Horse" by D. H. Lawrence. (Layout done in the spirit of the poem would have it a sprinkle of language centered on a blank page—as if drowning in, or freshly emerging from, the breathily empty and mystically charged potential of that whiteness. Like a brief poem as graffito on the side of Moby-Dick.)

13

"I am trying to find something out there beyond the place on which I have a footing," he said.

14

Ah!—all of the bi(and tri- and more)furcated lives!

Some few of them, essentially congruent and coeval—like the two lives of the androgyne; or time, in space; and space, in time.

Others, only tentatively partnered—like the couple in the cow suit at the masquerade.

And then, some as divergent as the halves of a split amoeba.

All of the gender benders, all of the pseudonyms and secret-agent incognitos, all of the schizophrenics, all of the demi-mortal sons and daughters of gods. . . .

All of the animal people; let's not forget the animal people.

꒩

The shaman (we *think* it's a shaman) in the (actual?) head (or mask?) of a stag or a bull (or something stag-like, something bull-like) has been with us as an image since the smoky, ocher pictures on the walls of the Paleolithic caves, and no doubt he (or she?) arrives there carried on a stream of species-minglement that goes back in unbroken form to the dawn-time when our own walk was a shamble, and our sleep, and our hunt, and our sex, partook of theirs.

The line between has always functioned as semipermeable. (With a seed in its shag, the bear becomes the portable sex of a fruit.) The line across which transformation occurs is with us, in us, down at the very weave of us. (Those micronanoparticles that change to *other* particles, "charm" or "up" or "taste" or "svelte" or "ookiness" or *whatever* they're being named these days.)

In *Man Into Wolf,* Robert Eisler says, "The prehistoric bone-sculpture known as the Venus of Brassempouy, and even more the well-known *Femme au renne* of Mas d'Azil and another male figure, are covered with lines which are clearly meant to indicate long hair covering the whole body." The body's own congenital hair, as on the Old Testament's wildly hirsute Esau?—or perhaps the hair of a cloak-like wraparound? (We have evidence—hide-scrapers of stone, near sewing needles of polished bone—that testify to a tailorly capability as far back as the Paleolithic.) Does it matter which? In either case, what counts is the sense of a *family* connection.

Herakles wears the skin of a lion; the American Indian medicine man, a buffalo robe (at times complete with head, hooves, tail). The emperor Nero "had himself sewn in the pelt of a wild beast," and in this costume "would proceed to attack the privy parts of men and women bound to stakes"—the costume as permission for this awful capability to rise forth from some cavity of Nero's, where it waited for this moment day and night. The Maenads of ancient Greece: a tribe (or "pack," more properly) of women who, as part of their rites, would hunt down men and children and tear them, literally tear them, into gore; these wore the signature pelts of wolf, of fox, of lynx. The same of the African cults of "leopard-men" and "panther-men." In all of these examples, the association is more than merely decorative; it says that the animal's power is taken on. We see it, still, in the form of comic-book characters: Wolverine; The Beast; The Human Tiger; Black Cat; Congorilla; etc. . . . a jungle's-worth of mighty heroes (plus, less likely yokings: Ant Man, Mole, The Wasp, Black Canary . . . these too are sentinels of justice.)

It's a very long cultural while since the eponymous father of masochists, Leopold von Sacher-Masoch, wrote the famed depiction of his own ideal dominating goddess, the "Venus in Furs," but it remains—that naked woman in her lustrous full-length sable coat—an icon of the erotic underworld even today. "Hey," we say, intending it as an observation on feral sexual grace, "that woman's *foxeee!*" And the *roué,* out to find a fitting lady love for his evening's entertainment?—even today, he's a "wolf."

Indeed, it's lupine imagery we've called upon most often, and it skulks along on the shadow side of our history without a stop—a relative we can't admit, but can't shake out of the bloodline.

"Thou hast become a wolf," *zikwa UR-BA-RA-aš ki-i-at*—the icy, stern words spoken to a captured outlaw, ostracizing him from human company, as far back as the ancient laws of the Hittites. One of Virgil's speakers says, in 39 B.C., "I have oft seen Moeras turn wolf by the aid of these herbs; he hides then in the woods, and calls out spirits from the depths of graves." Propertius mentions a spell that will alter a man to a wolf; and Petronius, in his *Satyricon,* tells of a man, Niceros, who watches a friend strip off his clothes and speak to the stars, and "all at once become a wolf, which ran off howling into the woods" and later attacked a herd of cattle. Pliny reports ("according to Euanthes") that the Arcadians chose, by lot, a man "who changed into a wolf and associated with wolves" in "a deserted place" for nine years; then they'd repeat the process. (I assume this means some sort of "scapewolf," whose amazing deportation siphoned away the community's ill luck.) The Arcadian king Lycaon, a "bitter tyrant, insane and foul," whose typical crimes include "an altar of human flesh," is finalized into the form he deserves by a punitive zap of one of Jove's thunderbolts: "then his jaws foamed, and his arms were forelegs." (Ovid and Plato refer to him.) And in Longus's *Daphnis and Chloe* we meet Dorcon, who, intent on raping Chloe, "took the skin of a great wolf and threw it over his shoulders," then hunkered down in the junipers, "having done his best to make of himself a beast"—how savvily apt a line. (At the same time, the second century A.D., Roman medical writer Marcellus Sidetes is already trying to wrestle the phenomenon out of the grips of myth and hearsay, and to study it instead as a psychological affliction . . . what he calls, and we'd still call today in our post-Freud world, lycanthropy.)

⌒

It skulks along on the shadow side of our history without a stop. "We had a werewolf scare in the winter of 1930": a farmer whose reputation includes the evil eye, whose cabin holds pin-stabbed wax manikins with the names of local honchos: "He was believed to walk by night as a wolf" (Pierre van Passen, *Days of Our Years*). "In 1960 Mr. Harold M. Young, proprietor of the zoo at Chiang Mai, Thailand, was hunting in the Lahu mountains when he encountered the locally dreaded 'taws,' a jungle werewolf"—this, from C. Dane's *The Occult in the Orient,* and it continues with the now familiar details: how the monster-beast was shot in the side, and its bloody trail followed to the hut of a man whose side is freshly shot(!) in [can you guess!] exactly the same spot(!). In the *Wichita Eagle* for August 26, 2001, is the front-page story of one Ric Banister, "a popular insurance agent, who doted on his son and daughter, and was a regular volunteer at church." Also, it seems, the perpetrator of up to thirteen robberies of banks in Kansas, Missouri, and Nebraska over a three-year period. Much is made in the paper's hyperventilating text about the "double life" this man led.

On a local TV news report, it's said that he never worked with an accomplice: "He was a lone wolf."

‿

Bogus? Factual? Both? In any case, it's everywhere. 1947: "There was a Navaho man in the neighborhood of the trading post at Klagaton, whom the other Navahos feared. He was called the Werewolf. He was believed to be able to turn himself into a wolf at night, and raid their flocks, and dig up the dead to rob their bodies of jewels. . . . The human wolf is a common and ancient belief of the Navahos" (Alberta Hannum, in *Spin a Silver Coin*).

It's everywhere, and it includes the especially designated "wolfs-head" squads of Nazi Germany, as well as the nurturing life that Kipling's Mowgli finds among his adoptive family in their bones-strewn cave: they look at the needy "man-cub" and their wolvish hearts go out to him in a way that the caring humanity of the innskeepers didn't extend to Mary and Joseph in *their* urgency. It heartens one a little to remember that the range of this extends beyond the murderous. A she-wolf suckled Romulus and Remus; and the wolf-raised girls of Midnapore, Bengal, are carefully documented (1942, *Wolf Children and Feral Man,* the Reverend J. Singh). I was a "Cub" Scout, we belonged to a "den," and our moms took turns as "den mother," and we swore to uphold the rules of the "pack," rules that were rooted in decency.

∽

"The five-fingered reptile has a plan of hand in general like ours. . . . Therefore the original sketch was made long ago" (Gustave Eckstein). "In loneliness a human being feels himself backward, down the long series of his avatars, into the earlier planetary life of animals, birds and reptiles and even into the cosmogonic life of rocks and stones" (John Cowper Powys).

Backward in time: a glissando of selves.

∽

And the ugly duckling awakes as a swan. The frog gets kissed, and—*whoops*—the princess is suddenly holding a randy handful of prince. Vampires. Centaurs. Pan. The pastor tends, one hopes with some adroitness, to his "flock." To Christ, all men are sheep. To Circe, they're all pigs. Korean peasant women "have often been witnessed suckling calves and piglets, after weaning their own babies." The Egyptian goddess Neith is represented suckling crocodiles. A "monkey-man" is reportedly on the rampage in Delhi: on May 17, 2001, the Delhi police "announced a reward of 50,000 rupees" if an offered tip led effectively to an arrest. We know that blood can spin at such a speed, it separates into two components: this might be the story of King Gilgamesh and his wild-man brother Enkidu, only in modern terms: the two of them as aspects of a single human psyche.

It's late afternoon, and Monica and Michael are attempting to tire out two-year-old Guthrie: maybe then he'll take his nap. A game of catch. Some play with Thomas the train. And then hand shadows on the child's bedroom wall. From the hand: a wolf. From the wolf: a goose—as if that barnyard fowl might rise new-minted as a phoenix, from the jaws of its demise. And from the goose: some undefinable and goofily knobbled glob. The child doesn't really care *what* shadow morphs forth from the parent's hand. The change itself is startling enough—the endless possibilities.

15

Sometimes a life of duality is forced on us from an out-side source. Says sizzling rock star Bono of the group U2: "At first, when you're reading stories about your life in the media—who you're supposedly sleeping with, how much money you're supposed to be making, what you had for breakfast—you feel violated. Then you start to realize that the person they're describing has very little to do with you, and is in fact much more interesting." (Wasn't that part of the Ran-man's story?—yielding to a "type" that fit his neighbors' early assumptions about him. And isn't it Albert Goldbarth, a stranger to Bono, who came up with "sizzling"?)

Sometimes, though, a life of opposing interior selves may be quite genuine—and still be denied with vehe-mence. When asked if "a bit of sex was implied" in his psalms and paeans, Whitman "replied unambiguously, *no*" (Michael Schmidt). Was it chiefly from his readers, or from himself, that his homoerotic yearnings needed to be so thoroughly locked away? The men are bathing in his poems, young, naked, joking in a public pond, the splash of their roughhousing arcing sharply into the air and then landing as tines of water dripping down over their shoulders, their chests, the rich tips of their nipples. *No,* the poet is saying, the venerable American bard. Their necks. Their forearms. *No,* and *no.*

Cecilia Payne-Gaposchkin, on her relation with Doro-thy Daglish (the teacher who, when Payne was thirteen, "recognized my passion for science and sympathized with it. She filled a unique place in my life . . .": "I am impatient now, as I was then, of the gross and cynical interpretations that are put upon the love of pupil for teacher. It is but one of the many forms of love."

⌣

And when Whitman volunteered his time in the wards of Washington Hospital, and the wounded of his country's strange, inverted war were brought in by the trainload, and he did what he could to comfort them in their unappeasable agonies, an apple for one, a hand held for another, or a letter to a sweetheart written down from someone's bloody-bubbled ramblings . . . what would he have thought, if footsoldier Harry T. Buford had been placed in the range of his ministering?

—Who "really" was Loreta Janeta Velasquez. When her husband, a young Confederate officer, left for the front in 1860, she left, too—without his knowing—and managed to enlist herself in his regiment under the Buford name. The apparatus she used had been carefully crafted: an old French army tailor in New Orleans created "half a dozen fine wire-net shields" to specification; these, below an undershirt of lisle thread and a series of cinchable chest straps, allowed her, as she said, "to disguise my features and readily pass as a man. But several points about my disguise I do not care to give to the public." Fair enough.

"I have successfully passed myself off as a man to thousands of keen-eyed observers. Many a time in camp I have gone to sleep with fifty or sixty officers, lying close together wrapped in our blankets, without fear of detection."

In fact, "fear was a word I did not know the meaning of," and here she refers to the fear of battle. If anything, she had an active appetite for the field of war. Early on, her husband was killed when his rifle accidentally exploded—a stupid and embarrassing death—and Loreta, abrim with Confederate patriotism, determined to stay with the troops; shortly after, she took part in the battle of Bull Run, helping rout the enemy and earning General Stonewall Jackson's special recommendation for promotion.

She spied behind Union lines, she served as a block-ade-runner, she accepted her turn digging trenches out of the skillet-hard dirts of winter, she took avid part in the nightmare confrontation out at Fort Donelson in February of 1862: "I could face the cannon better than the cries of the wounded. Every now and then a shriek would be uttered that would strike terror to my soul. The battle raged on. [It lasted four days.] My clothes were perfectly stiff with ice and I ached in every limb, but by a resolute effort I stood my ground."

C. J. S. Thompson: "It is said to have been the most terrible battle of the war. In many of the trenches Loreta saw the bodies heaped together six or seven feet high."

Plus, *Newsweek* on the Olympics: "A Polish sprinter was stripped of her 1964 gold and bronze medals after failing a sex test in 1967, and the 1932 gold medalist in the 100-meter dash was found, at her autopsy in 1980, to have testes."

This year, Wal-Mart was ordered "to pay more than two million dollars to a transsexual ex-employee who claimed he was fired after his boss learned he was a man."

⌢

We wake, we've crossed a stream eight hours wide—eight hours of unknown else-life. What gets lost?—or gets accumulated? How many streams, over how many days, until there's a recognizable difference? Sometimes light's a wave; sometimes a bolus. Who are *we,* to be immutable? We wake, we look: is this my hand in the morning sun? And next to me, here: is this the same person I married? Everybody gets to ask that question. Fair enough.

∿

And: after her death, he sorted her belongings. In the trunk of her car—photos, letters. He couldn't believe it. She had another family; a husband, a child. She'd stay with them one weekend a month, when the office sent her to Abbeyville. It was real. How could it be?—but it was real. He read through the letters again. His name was Ed; the little girl was six, her name was Traci Leigh.

And: once, okay; twice, a fight; three times, and that bastard was history, and he'd hit that magic number last night, so now, while he was out for a while, she started to pack his things, and in the bottom drawer, beneath his socks and a box he called his coin collection, there was a package . . . Polaroid photos, some receipts. She spent the next two hours on the floor right there, dry heaving their history out of her, down to the last sea-bottom worm and squirming trilobite.

Not that it has to be so bleak. Across town, in another house, in a bedroom soft with candlelight, a man looks at his sleeping wife . . . he's still astounded, hours after the fact. That afternoon!—he's known her intimately for ten years, but he never knew she had such . . . what? . . .

nobility, such nobility inside, that he saw float out of her that day with the natural grace of an air-swept cotton-wood seed.

ᴖ

We slough our skins, we mimic out patchy backgrounds, we regenerate. We may as well be claymation figures.

"For ten years we lived together in bliss" (Elena Alvarez of Lima, Peru). And then the police appeared at their door: her husband Juan-Miguel was charged "with the slayings of twenty-four girls in Argentina, Ecuador, Paraguay and Peru." He had a salesman job that took him throughout South America—"and every time that he came back home, he brought me a new piece of jewelry."

And then there's Russell Keys, who traveled from London to Phoenix, Arizona, to marry the woman he'd met through a classified ad. He wouldn't hurt a fly . . . but suffered from a mental condition that made him confess to imagined crimes. He told Dominique he *was* a serial killer . . . "shallow graves" . . . "five women." The afternoon of July 21, 2001, she shot him to death . . . twice in the chest and once in the hip, and the world was safe at last from this sad, harmless, overblown bag of a man and his sadly dichotomized dreamlife.

In a *Far Side* cartoon, there's a snake—let's call him Mr. Snake—in his middle-class bedroom, wearing some kind of tight mesh thing, that goes from his bottommost tip to what we'd term, if he were a person, his neck. And in the suddenly opened doorway, Mrs. Snake, with her bouffant hair and eyeglasses, screams out, "Oh my God, Bernie! You're wearing my nylon?"

Here's a more everyday version. A couple's asleep.

Their sweat has dried by now. They lightly touch each other. On the bedside stand is a book—a novel, *Gatherer of Clouds* by Sean Russell. The bookmark is at page 403: "Coming to a tree trunk that curved out almost horizontally over the water, Shonto stopped and leaned against it. Nishima circled its base and leaned against the opposite side. . . . They stayed like that, side by side facing opposite directions."

Outside their window, it's nearly dawn: the sky is just beginning to declare itself as separate from the ground. These form two grayish shapes, in shades of char and pearl, that blend and don't blend, like the two tiers in some Rothko paintings.

Downstairs, in the refrigerator, the vinaigrette is busy becoming a clear, light-amber half on top, and a deeper, more marrowy underhalf.

16

—A most reasonable self-survey, on occasion.

In the mail today I received the current catalogue of a company that specializes in antique toys. On page 8 is a "nineteenth-century German clown toy," smiling out at me from his color photograph, festively indicating good fellowship and a beckoning wealth of belly laughs. "Pull the string and the devil pops out of his head." With one of these, a person could practice the skills of exorcism a dozen times a day, as needed. I think Eliza would understand.

And what does hopeless goofus Steven Nelson see looking out of his mirror—the fat shnozz and the meek gaze of a man who seems predestined for a KICK ME sticker slapped onto his butt? Maybe. Surely. Then again, when his Tiger Siren Wrist Communicator beeps, he's ready to tear his shirt apart to reveal the orange-and-ebony-stripe insignia on the chest of his crime-fighter underwear: a subtle but macho ferocity is his, now that he's . . . Tiger Man! The parting of that white shirt (and he must go through a hundred a month) is every bit as shocking as the curtains on the stage of the annual Church League Children's Christmas Carol Competition opening to reveal Deacon Mulligrew's wife and the choirmaster fucking like animals. Who *is* ever comfortable 100 percent with the personal zoo that paces back and forth behind the rib cage?

Answer: Dennis Abner, forty-three-year-old ex-Marine

and currently San Diego computer programmer, who's spent something over 2,000 hours in tattoo parlors, to have himself striped like a Bengal tiger ("My whole body is one pastiche of stripes and shading"). "His upper lip is reconstructed with silicon to give him the classic cat-shaped mouth and his teeth have been filed to razor-sharp fangs, his fingernails grown out to claws. His mane of hair is dyed orange, and he wears greenish contact lenses with slit-like irises, to give his eyes a jungle-cat appearance. Twelve six-inch-long whiskers (fiberglass) have been permanently implanted in Dennis' face and they sweep proudly, regally out of his upper lip."—This, after a "vision dream" two decades ago in which a voice instructed him "to follow the ways of the tiger."

At the moment, his plans include—at the cost of another $100,000—having "actual tiger fur grafted onto every inch of my body." I'm reminded of a statement in Clifford D. Simak's science-fiction novel *Shakespeare's Planet,* referred to as well in one of my earlier footnotes. Horton, the protagonist, has gone through . . . well, there's no need to summarize his starways-spanning odyssey, but in chapter 22, "there seemed two of him, although the twoness of him seemed not inconvenient and even natural."

17

September 1996: "Makhsud Shafigi is the only person left in the world who can speak Chagatai, the court language of the Mongols in the 13th century" *(The Fortean Times).*

He speaks, and his words are carried from their springs of original meaning, out into the limitless ocean of gibberish. . . .

Of unidentifiable parts of bodies in news reports, there is no limit. Of vagrant portions of bodies, there is no end. Of fragments of the holy and of the infamous, no vault could hold them all in congregation.

The relics of Saint Thérèse (the "Little Flower" and one of just three women ever to be declared a "Doctor of the Church") have been on continuous tour since 1997, in a reliquary of jacaranda wood and gold that weighs 400 pounds and is transported by a customized silver bus called "the Thérèsemobile."

Some of us place a not dissimilar value on our own dear partite flesh. The fingers (five) and toes (all ten) that Major Michael "Bronco" Lane lost due to frostbite climbing Everest, he donated to the National Army Museum in London. Champagne. Speeches. Video zooms. The Science Museum in London is the recipient of Robert Moss's heart, "three times the usual size, from childhood rheumatic fever"—fitted with a new heart, he endowed his country with ownership of the old.

And fitted successfully with a transplant hand and forearm (having lost his own in a firecracker explosion in 1985), former paramedic Matthew Scott is joyous— even though the hand, in its original life, belonged to a man "who used it to shoot his former wife and girlfriend and then, when he was convicted, himself." Scott is the second person to have had this kind of transplant. But Clint Hallam, the first, eventually complained that he was "mentally detached" from his new hand, it was "too big and pink," and he's searched so far through both the United States and France for a surgeon willing to amputate.

(On the subject of miracle medical replacements, we should also note the mummy of a woman with a wooden—and very elegantly shaped— big toe: her own was amputated due to gangrene. And I don't know *why* assigning a date to this should add to our amazement, but it does: 1000 B.C., approximately. A wooden toe, long, slim, and durable, of expert engineering, from a thousand years before the feet of Christ trod Galilee. It would outweigh that leg of Ahab's in the balance-pans of simple, oh-wow wonder.

As, I'd wager, would the penis of an unnamed man from Tiflis, Georgia. Cancer took his first one, and his second is "one of his middle fingers, complete with knuckles." Twelve days after the seventeen-hour operation, he was able to urinate "via a tube inside the new organ, and a year after that, two girlfriends of his were said to be 'more than satisfied with the results.'")

But when Eliza says she "used to daydream tripping

over body parts," she means those stories of litter-like pieces *without* a knowable provenance. Of these, the empty inches and/or minutes at a shift's end in the newsrooms of the world are filled without cease from a never-failing fount of global weirdness.

A woman in São Paulo, Brazil discovered a finger in a bag of popcorn. (Maybe for a second she reduplicated the pose of God and Adam on the Sistine Chapel ceiling.) A student spat out a thumb in a high-school cafeteria in Hyannis, Massachusetts: it was cramped inside a sandwich he had purchased, worse than a mealworm. The lawsuit jokes of late-night talk-show monologues begin with just such errant thumbs as that. At a Bellevue, Washington apartment complex, a janitor noticed a knot of crows "pecking at something" dropped on the parking tarmac. Yes: a human thumb; and yes: of unguessable origin; "in good shape," says the *Seattle Times,* "except for scattered peck marks."

And of thievery, the *Norwich* (Connecticut) *Bulletin* bears these cautionary words: "A Massachusetts man was arrested Friday at Foxwoods Resort Casino and charged with stealing two human corneas." Of thievery, the British *Sunday Mail* reports: "One thousand cats' eyes were stolen from the busy A75 Cretna-Stranraer Euro-route in Scotland." Yes; for every year (approximately) between the life of Christ and the time of that deeply teak brown, carpentered toe: one stolen Scottish cat eye.

And the skull D.C. police "found at a Washington house in a drug raid"; they "believe it was being used to put a hex on a D.C. Superior Court judge." And the "witch bottle" (thick, green-muddy glass) discovered "with its contents intact despite being buried for more than 270 years inside some house foundations near the castle in Reigate, Surrey." Organic chemist Alan Massey described its contents: "Human urine, pubic hairs, an eyelash and eight bent brass pins." Meaning—? "Bending the pins was a way for them of symbolically killing the witch."

Doc Killed Wife, Cut Up Body, Threw Pieces From His Plane ("He was a respected plastic surgeon who often traveled into Mexico to perform free surgeries there on underprivileged children"). *Body of Naked, Hooded Customer Is Cut into Pieces After He Dies Waiting for a Dominatrix Spanking* ("Asher admits she and a boyfriend butchered the body with a saw, then stuffed the parts inside eight double-liner garbage bags and dumped them in a landfill"). *Palestinian Kills Self and 3 Israelis* ("'It was horrible, just horrible,' said William Weiss, a municipal worker. 'There were hands, legs, flesh, and a head thrown around. It turned out that was apparently the terrorist's head'").

Enough. Enough.

‿

Although megastars insure parts of themselves for staggering sums (dance master Michael Flatley's legs at 47.5 million dollars; Janet Jackson's butt at 22.5; or Dolly Parton's bust at "a modest $481,000"), "sometimes they don't have what it takes to do an attractive close-up," says an acquaintance of mine—her name withheld—whose own six-figure salary last year was earned as a "body double": "usually my toes or my tits. So when you see a flash of [Big-deal Diva's] chest up on the screen?—c'est moi."

And from the realm of tacky Q&A in *Wichita Eagle's* syndicated Sunday magazine, *Parade:* "Did actor David Duchovny use a 'butt double' for the scene in *Evolution* where he drops his pants and bares his bottom?" J. R. C. from Philadelphia, Pennsylvania, needs to know. Well he didn't! Those buns were truly his own buns, Ms. or Mr. C.—although by now the understanding that a part of X may not, upon inspection, "really" be a part of "X" is our inheritance; was even old by the long-gone time of that prosthetic wooden toe (which has the look of lovely folk art now, and not of practical necessity) and certainly was ancient in the days when sun and candlelight were glimmers on the gold replacement nose strapped to the empty space on the face of astronomer Tycho Brahe (let *that* be a lesson for the rest of us, on the foolishness of drunken, youthful dueling in an alley).

⌒

An Afghanistan scene, as reported in *Newsweek:* "countless maimed victims of land mines who rush to catch the prosthetic legs that parachute through the skies from Red Cross planes."

And what would Ahab make of that, what dream would he think he'd wandered into, witnessing such hell-wrought beauty?—hundreds of legs floating down from the heavens, each with its own guiding flower.

⌒

Eliza's dream: a single wing in the sky. A wing that's canted into the wind. One wing: a wing alone.

It could be angels, ghosts, and UFOs are just a thin slice we're attuned to see (like visible light), which comes to our awareness from totalities (like the whole of the spectrum) that, themselves, are normally undetectable by our everyday senses.

Eliza's dream: a thumb—and nothing else. A thumb with its whorls in the shape of the opaque gaze of the Sphinx: uncompromising; something outside of the boundaries of sequential time.

A thumb with amnesia: where? how? whose?

A thumb hitchhiking, out of the fog of the past and into the clotted haze of the future.

18

In the children's fantasy novel *Half Magic* by Edward Eager, the mother says, "There's only one explanation. I must have lost my memory, just for a minute."

To which "the rather small gentleman" Mr. Smith replies, correcting her, "Oh, there's never only *one* explanation. It depends on which one you want to believe."

19

And every editor (although some with a delicate touch).

In his "Introduction" to *The Sayings of Samuel Pepys,* the editor, Richard Ollard, offers this: "Pepys's characteristic expression is not epigrammatic. Capable as he was of pithy, witty, searching remarks, his preference was for the orotund, the long, unhurried sentence branching off into parentheses, but always rejoining a main clause that is often coterminus with a paragraph. I have sometimes butchered these. . . ."

20

In one of the nuttier Legion of Super-Heroes plots (*Adventure Comics,* May 1965), the luckless Lightning Lad's right arm is lost to the "Super-Moby Dick of Space." (And you thought *you* had insufferable workdays.)

Eric Brown: "His character then took on a bitter, revengeful edge for the rest of that issue, before becoming hopeful at the prospect of someday having the arm regrown."

⌣

As for prosthetic legs . . . when Mildred the preying mantis lost her lower left forelimb, "math teacher and amateur insect expert Robin Nagy" fashioned her a new forelimb from the bristle of "a household cleaning brush."

He's shown with a jeweler's loupe in one eye, gingerly holding his leaf green patient: "Gluing the new limb in place was very tricky."

Now she uses it to catch baby locusts and beetle larvae, and "cleans it like it were a real leg."

21

In 1900—the year that both Cecilia Payne and the century were born—a forty-two-year-old German mathematician named Max Planck wrote an equation, $E=hv,$ which (as one authority puts it, echoing most) "was the beginning of quantum theory."

Planck would not have seen himself as a firebrand radical, not in science or anywhere else—he was, another source says, "a pillar of nineteenth-century German high culture"—and yet in order to account for certain energy-spectrum phenomena, he needed to hypothesize that energy is emitted not continuously, but in what Planck called *quanta:* unconnected units. With this single understanding, classical physics started its rapid obsolescing. Nothing could be the same from that moment. Shortly, Niels Bohr was mapping the interior disappearing acts of the atom, Werner Heisenberg was studying the wondrous shoulder-shrug of indeterminacy. Quarks. Anti-matter.

Planck was involved in a number of telling occasions. As the active editorial director of *Annals of Physics* in the seminal year of 1905, he recognized at once the cosmos-shaking implications of a paper on relativity submitted by a young man, Albert Einstein. "The age of Newton was over. Science was something else now." It was Planck, in fact, who applied the word "relativity" to the theory—Einstein neither coined the term nor thought to use it in his first descriptions.

Yes, but for all of his subsequent contributions,

Planck's most formative achievement—it's the one that led us into our rich, idea-yeasty, risky twentieth-century physics—still remains his insight of 1900, when the given-wisdom structure of a universe without leaps was completely and (so far) forever destroyed.

—Which is to say, Eliza was right. There *are* gaps. There are strange, incomprehensible lacunae. Reality blinks: we don't know *what* takes place in those betweens. We shirk from acknowledging this, we shrink from its inhuman implications. But there *are* gaps; not that we're meant to stare at them long, any more than at sunspots.

∼

The National Examiner: "Fifty-eight-year-old granny Betty Lou Montague was a bingo player, doll collector, church raffle pie baker, rescue squad volunteer, VFW and Elks lodge waitress, holiday charity chairwoman— and a cold-blooded killer, say cops. At a Virginia State Police barracks in Wytheville, she confessed to two murders." She was nabbed while—get this—"going from neighbor to neighbor collecting contributions for one of her victims' burial plots."

Does it make *any* sense to suggest that she is (and that anybody *could* be, perhaps) a humanscopic version of submicroscopic yes-no, here-there, somewhere-nowhere quantum flux?—that she exists at one "time" in two "states"?

22

"Desecrated as the body is, a vengeful ghost survives and hovers over it" (Melville, taking the killing of a whale to its last degree).

Are ectoplasmic presences apportioned to the sizes of the bodies that engender them?

In tomb art of sarcophagi, there's often a *ka*—a kind of ancient Egyptian soul— that sculls the air above the casket, hovering there, about the size of a small hawk.

Then . . . above the bloodied waters where a whale died? What bird could be enough? What roc from out of the *Arabian Nights* could be enough?

A cloud might do; a cloud that holds the whole of a season's weather. If it's stained dark with a tinge of mammalian life. And if it's tied to this spot in the sea by an atomic string of empathy.

In *Hamlet,* that most ghost-weighted play, a cloud is very like a whale.

23

Women aren't alone in these straits. Men account for approximately 1 percent of mastectomies and cystectomies-with-radiation. (And tumors tend to be diagnosed at a more advanced stage in male patients, making them even more potentially fatal.) But this flip side of the cancer coin is rarely addressed in public. One popular lay text on the disease, for example, "is written for women"(and authored by three), and so "we have not expounded on the treatment of males." That's it; *adiós.*—Needlessly exclusionary, it seems to me, since only a few more pages might have made the book (and compassionately so) more democratic.

But no prejudice or inhibition blocked my student Child of Glory ("I *know* the roster printout says Les Smith. But now my name is Child of Glory.") from his first week's turning in of work, a *looong* confessional opus: "My Mastectomy." Three hundred pounds of flan white bounce, a broadly Slavic-Midwest face, and a small bright tribe-of-Islam cap on the top of his head like a windup knob . . . you wouldn't think he needed this additional tragicomic gilding.

Some quotes:

When I was a freshman in college I was cast
As the female lead in a short Three Act play.
Now, it seemed, I had been similarly selected.
. . . .

The surgeon cut deeper, ever deeper,
Chunks of flesh and muscle were cut out of my chest.
Waiting . . . waiting . . . waiting for the results.
Malignant—such a desperate sounding word.
. . . .
Even my family, tears falling like a soft rain,
Came to tell me that I did great and that they loved me.
I had always wanted my family to come to one of my
        shows, and now they had.
. . . .
And so, I drifted off into a demerol-induced dream,
Dreaming of standing in front of a full-length mirror
        and knowing
At last that I was beautiful and touchable.

He missed the second week of class because, as he
told me in confidence during the third, "I needed a little
mental rest in a mental-rest place." He was gone once
more for the fourth week of class; and I never saw Child
of Glory again.

24

Even a man who is pure of heart
And says his prayers at night
May become a wolf
When the wolfbane blooms
And the autumn moon is bright.

   —Curt Siodmak, from his script for *The Wolf Man*
    (Universal Pictures, 1941); as recited by Maria
    Ouspenskaya as "the gypsy woman"

25

A final favorite: the "interesting case of the great violinist Fritz Kreisler, who confessed in February 1935 that he had been playing his own compositions for thirty years, but ascribing them to such early masters as Vivaldi, Couperin, Porpora, Pugnani and Padre Martini" (Marston Bates).

26

Not that Doctor Vettius is necessarily culpable as the instigator. "Messalina apparently possessed," says William B. Klingaman, "a voracious carnal appetite." The ancient Roman satirist Juvenal writes of the nights she would sneak from the palace, hooded, rouged, and "under an ash-blonde wig" to work in the cubby of a brothel, where—to entice a clientele—she would strip, "displaying her gilded nipples and the belly that once housed a prince of the blood." And Pliny tells of when she "chose to compete against a certain well-loved prostitute and, over a twenty-four-hour period, beat her record by bedding twenty-five men." It may be safest to infer that the dynamic here between physician and patient was one of complicity.

27

Even Marco Polo's famous islands—Male Island and Female Island, thirty miles apart—admit a ritual congress. For although on Male Island "the men do not live with their wives or with any other women; but all the women live on the other island" . . . even so, "the men of Male Island go over to Female Island for three months of March and April and May," and then "they sow the corn, which the women will till and reap" (as well, of course, as sowing children, which the women will raise; the boys, at fourteen, being shipped to Male Island, someplace that I've always seen in my mind as a mix of monastery and frat house).

There are couples who have held a frigid silence over years, such was their enmity, and even so, as physics knows: the cold is an able conductor.

I could list a cornucopia of blended states—from twilight to that atom on the dial where Reverend Do-Good's Spirit of Jesus Hour and Mistress Exotica's Call-In Sex Chat touch enough to be a cotyledon of zinging megahertz—but would it finally (this is the test) be anything *near* persuasive enough to counter the bedrock insularity Thackeray so energetically posits?

> Thus, O friendly readers, we see how every man
> in the world has his own private griefs and busi-
> ness, by which he is more cast down or occupied
> than by the affairs or sorrows of any other

person. . . . You and your wife have pressed the same pillow for forty years and fancy yourselves united.—Psha, does she cry out when you have the gout, or do you lie awake when she has the toothache? . . . Ah, sir—a distinct universe walks about under your hat and under mine.

28

In 1919—the same year in which Max Planck received the Nobel Prize for fathering quantum physics, and Sir Arthur Stanley Eddington voyaged down to Brazil for astronomical sightings that provided corroboration of Einstein's theory of relativity—Ray Cummings published a 22,000-word science-fantasy novelette, "The Girl in the Golden Atom" (he had originally called it "The Girl in the Ring": his editor nixed that), in *All-Story Weekly,* the home of Edgar Rice Burroughs's Tarzan and Martian adventures.

Cummings was born on the same day as Thomas Edison, and for five years worked for the Edison office, editing newsletters, writing copy for Edison studio recordings, and the like. But in 1919 he left, and devoted himself from then on to his fiction—this, in large part due to the huge success of "The Girl in the Golden Atom" (which in 1922 was liberated from pulp, reprinted as a hardcover novel by Harper & Brothers and, in England, by Methuen: for a "scientific romance" of that time, this was close to apotheosis). Certainly *something* of his Edison days adhered to Cummings: his books are enticingly gadgeted with early versions of robots, spaceships, time machines, etc. In "The Girl in the Golden Atom," its hero—referred to only as "the Chemist"—invents a pill that will shrink him infinitely, and another that will expand him back to normal.

And why? It's the oldest story. He shares it one night

at his private club, with his three friends, the Doctor, the Big Business Man, and the Very Young Man. There are drinks and cigars and an air of manly confidentiality, and the Chemist relates how his belief in the smallness of things (why, even the atom, he tells them, isn't the limit of "small"!) encouraged him to spend four years in the search for a microscope lens that would penetrate into the farthest subrecesses of matter.

"'I glanced around for some object to examine. On my finger I had a ring, my mother's wedding ring, and I decided to use that. I have it here.' He took a plain gold band from his finger and laid it on the table." Then he points out a tiny scratch on one side. "'This is the place into which I looked.'"

The scratch becomes a canyon. And in it, a cave. In *it*, a pool. And beside the pool (and this beats the observation of electrons and protons by a zillionfold): a woman of pinup appeal, a woman "'beautiful, according to our own standards of beauty; her long braided hair a glowing black; her face, delicate of feature and winsome in expression. Her lips were a deep red. She was dressed only in a short tunic. She seemed to be singing. She danced with the wild grace of a wood nymph.

'I knew at last that the scientific achievement I had made counted for little with me. It was the girl. I realized then that the only being I ever could care for was living out her life with her world, and, indeed, her whole universe, inside an atom of that ring.'"

Hence, his next scientific triumph: two new chemicals, in pill form, one that will shrink him to an appropriate diminution, and a second to reverse the effect. The narrative then addresses a few of the easier complications:

yes, those objects that are in contact with his body—his clothes, the vials of pills—will undergo commensurate shrinkage; yes, time-flow is differently felt in the micro-world, so a man can have his week of high adventure there and still be back in a private club in Manhattan in what seems a matter of hours. The Chemist's final question—will his good friends hold a continuous watch in this room, safeguarding the ring, until he returns from its golden innerspace?—is met with three resounding Yesses. And thus does the journey begin.

And thus, the story: of love pursued, and hindered, and won (the Chemist introduces kissing, hitherto unknown, into this world); of good (the beautiful woman's people—her name, lyrically, is Lylda) versus evil (a totalitarian martial state, the Malites—reducing the fascist troopers of 1914 Edison Studio newsreels to the level of atom-size bad guys); and of a stalwart defender ("I was considered by Lylda somewhat in the light of a Messiah, come to save her nation").

And he indeed *does* act the role of a savior; and he *will* make one return trip to New York on his own, to verify the safety of such passage, and then go back into the ring for the lithesome Lylda, to fetch her (duly expandable) home with him from her own birthplace that could fit a million times over into a mote of dust. Finally, the results of the Chemist's great scientific discovery are presented as sweet smooches and some scenes of lively battle—this great scientific discovery that the Doctor at one point says (without indication of humor or irony) is "almost too big an idea to grasp."

ᔕ

Nobel-level science—the actual rational, impartially and repeatedly tested, nonpartisan Galileo-and-Pasteur thing—as well as practical gizmory of the kind that builds us better mousetraps and chimney flues, have always held palaver along one edge of themselves with the iffier domain of what today we call "junk science." Even Newton, that prince of enlightened cognition, seriously investigated astrology—he was willing to give it the same consideration he laved upon thermodynamics. Edison, says Wendy Kaminer, "was attracted to the occult and various paranormal phenomenon. He believed in psychokinesis (the telepathic control of physical objects) and tried to invent a machine for communicating electronically with the dead." It's tempting to see a young Ray Cummings tiptoe past a laboratory room in which his boss is rapt in thinking: copper? gossamer? catgut? zinc?—which strand will best conduct his words to the afterlife of the wandering shades?

Late in the twentieth century, it was Max Planck's theory of quantum mechanics—cheapened into a party buzzword—that became especially liable to abuse by the fuzzy-of-thinking and the chicanerously manipulative. Kaminer: "The more limited your understanding of science, the more that scientists resemble masters of the occult, and the more that paranormal phenomena seem likely to reflect undiscovered scientific truths. Meaningless references to quantum physics pervade New Age literature. By indiscriminate use of the word 'quantum,' [New Age guru] Deepak Chopra appropriates the authority and sophistication of physics, referring offhandedly to the 'quantum nature of exercise,' or offering to lead you into 'quantum space' and even 'beyond the quantum, where old age, senility, infirmity, and death do not exist,'" which is baloney, malarkey, gibberish, snake oil, doublespeak, the poop of the bull.

ꙮ

As a game, however, it's fun to set serious physics like a grid atop the derring-do antics of Cummings's protagonist; and the terms we use today that are honorific of Planck are particularly conducive to this.

John Gribbin: "Quantum theory tells us that no measurable quantity can be completely smooth and continuous. The 'Planck length' is the length scale at which space itself is grainy." Think of it: *space itself is grainy!* We can imagine that, if we were Deepak Chopras of the adventure novel, this would be a dandy explanation for the series of subuniverses Cummings's Chemist describes.

"'Planck time' is the smallest unit of time that can exist (the shortest tick on the cosmic clock)." And that would no doubt be the time and the clocks of Lylda's people. Or, as Timothy Ferris says, "In the very early universe— during the 'Planck epoch'—there was no 'arrow of time,' so it would be meaningless to talk of something as having come 'before.' Hence no problem of temporal regress arises." A *week,* the Chemist spends in Lylda's lovey-dovey company, instructing her in courtship, and reducing her foes to a ragtag straggle. His three friends, though, will confirm that he's back in New York within just forty hours.

ꙮ

Fourteen-year-old twins Vitalija and Vilija Tamuleviciutes are smiling out at me from a photograph in this news magazine: they're giving me V-for-Victory signs, two pretty girls with vivid auburn hair in straight bangs, on a sunny day.

They were born joined at the tops of their heads—so completely, they look in *those* photos as if they're really one single long segmented creature. It wasn't until age two that they were surgically disconnected: "Doctors carefully cut apart the brain tissue the little girls shared." Each lost one-third of her skull in the process; then it wasn't for another two years that each, in an individual twelve-hour process, had her skull reformed. "They are now normal, lively teenagers. Mercifully, they have no memory of those earliest years."

Separated. . . . I'm thinking of—what's the title of that Disney "Donald Duck" cartoon?—the one where he's considering playing hooky from school, and a thumbling devil-Donald-Duck appears in a *poof* on one of his shoulders, whispering temptation into that ear; while on the other shoulder, a thumbling angel-Donald-Duck is whispering a countervailing paean to the moral life. As if our famous drake had been spun in a Tilt-A-Whirl, and his two essential plasmas wound up staring at one another.

Everybody: good-self, bad-self. There's a distant hinge of connectedness, but *so* far back in time, "they have no memory of those earliest years." The same with matter and radiation. The atom of Cummings; the atom of Planck.

29

Cecilia Payne-Gaposchkin's daughter, on her mother: "She had tremendous nostalgia for family heirlooms, and she suffered agonies if a china cup or dish was broken."

30

Can our quotidian bits of loss lay claim—on a subjective plane—to mythic grandeur?

This is what Eliza felt:

"And now, concentric circles seized the lone boat itself, and all its crew, and each floating oar, and every lance-pole, and spinning, animate and inanimate, all round and round in one vortex, carried the smallest ship of the Pequod out of sight . . . and the great shroud of the sea rolled on as it rolled five thousand years ago" (Melville, the ending of *Moby-Dick*).

31

National Organization of Circumcision Information Resource Centers, Natural Organization of Restoring Men, National Organization to Halt the Abuse and Routine Mutiliation of Males, etc.

32

I quote from Allen Edwardes's *Erotica Judaica*. The full sentence—what an astonishing choice of verb!—begins: "And the campsite where the Hebrews cut this covenant with Yahweh was thereafter known as *Gilgil* . . . ," etc.

33

Stone Walls doe not a Prison make,
Nor I'ron bars a Cage.
> —from Richard Lovelace,
>   "To Althea, from Prison," 1649

34

Leslie Fiedler suggests that, since Jack London may have been warned by his doctors of "how little time he had left" (and he did die in 1916, one year after *The Star Rover's* publication), he probably "identified with the condemned men in Death's Row, who . . . endure the special torture of knowing when and how their deaths will come."

In any case, he certainly suffered from multiple physical ailments as he wrote the book, as well as from "a gradual loss of mobility and a growing sense of isolation." Fiedler reasons persuasively that this "made him [especially] responsive to all images of constriction and loneliness."

There may have been times when a single creature, Darrell Jack Standing London, was at work on those pages, willing not only the rising of the next word, then the next, but also willing the rising of disembodied consciousness out of the difficult chrysalis living had become.

⌒

And what about Marion Nostwick?—thirty-three, who'd been told she was dying and, with the kind of focus some people *do* manage to forge for themselves in dire circumstances, planned her funeral service down to the hymns, and who'd sing what, and when, and the floral arrangements, and sealed notes of good-bye to her husband

Doug, three children, two beloved pet Dobermans, and twenty-seven friends.

The doctors, though, had mixed up patients' files. She'd spent three months living through another, unknown person's dying, and then was given back her original future, whatever it was.

Three months, spent gingerly walking on the edge of the world and staring into the shoreless roils of mist she thought she could reach out and touch; or not "touch," no . . . "dissolve into."

What word does she bring, now that she's back with us, from farther away than the astronauts who golfed on the moon?

What contrapuntal wisdom?

"I am here, there, everywhere, nowhere" (Charles Dickens).

35

The association of satellites or islands with voluptuaries' loungeabouts and robbers' roosts and utopian hippie communities and pirate radio stations and hermetic religious promised lands and tax evaders' free states . . . has a long and crowded history. From the hook-'em-in back cover of a 1958 sci-fi novel, *Starhaven* by Robert Silverberg (under his pseudonym Ivar Jorgenson): "After seven years of beachcombing on the pleasure planet of Mulciber, Johnny Mantell was unjustly accused of murder. Johnny had to get out. And the only place for an outcast like himself was the impregnable outlaw world of Starhaven, a refuge that defied all galactic laws." The Pilgrim fathers may optimistically have thought of America in just such sanctuarial terms.

Often, these islands are so removed from normality and dailiness, they take on the stamp of the eldritch: the Mysterious Lands, the Misty Isles, the Unknown Places, etc. Melville marries both permissions—that for piracy, and that for supernatural occasion—when he quotes (and later comments on) the account of the buccaneer Cowley, who discovered an island hideout for his crew: "'My fancy led me to call it Cowley's Enchanted Isle, for, we having had a sight of it upon several points of the compass, it appeared always in so many different forms; sometimes like a ruined fortification; upon another point like a great city,' etc.

"That Cowley linked his name with this self-transforming isle suggests the possibility that it conveyed to him some meditative image of himself."

⌣

Favorite titles of mine from among their ilk: *Islandia* by Austin Tappan Wright, *The Island of Doctor Moreau* by H. G. Wells, and *Penguin Island* by Anatole France. All of these invented locales exist somewhere outside of the standard circumference of things. As do, for example, the "real" Polynesian islands so lushly depicted in Melville's *Omoo* and *Typee:* their fronds and fish and coconuts of an almost preternatural size and silkiness; their waterfalls as stupendous as something come to Earth from the bands of the constellations; and their innocently naked nut brown island men and women, whose days seem filled with what we'd call "disporting" and "frolicing." (Gauguin's retreat to this same world, and his record of it in *Noa Noa,* also come to mind.)

I like to think these drifting asterisks to the main text of our human condition are often the sites of hermitages, where donnish contemplation, yogic mantra-chanting, occur in an azure tranquility. Maybe so—for some. Of course "extremity" has no single dominant tenor; and when the island of Tasmania was first colonized by Britain in the early 1800s, it gave rise to numberless horrors. Paul Johnson tells us that "a convict called Charles Routley, with an iron hook instead of a hand, escaped from the harbor, murdered six men, sewed the body of one of them in a bullock's skin, roasted it and ate it and, when finally run down, waved his iron hook in the dock and cursed God and man."

Certainly Tasmania's aboriginal population was cursed. Within two generations of Europe's invasion, they had been—the entire 5,000 of them—exterminated.

⌒

And we know that Robert Silverberg—when his other self Ivar Jorgenson had completed a chapter of *Starhaven* on some night before the rent was due—became his *other* other self, Dan Eliot, author of *Backstage Sinner, Lust Cult, Sin Sink, Sex Bait, Passion Partners,* and an ogleable host of other one-night porno wonders. He was also Loren Beauchamp, author of lesbian erotica like 1962's *Strange Delights.* It's fair to suggest each pseudonym was an island of anonymity he retreated to. And it's tempting to guess that Loren Beauchamp was very aware that the first of the poignant lesbian singers—Sappho herself, poet and now icon—made an island her home.

36

Much is made of Dickens's composite psychology—both as person and as artist.

In the worlds he created, every type and part-type and anomaly appears to be represented with the vapor of persuasive detail shimmying off the skin. "An amazing word, *Dickensian*. It's extraordinary how one man could inspire an adjective with dozens of meanings, many of which are contradictory" (Norrie Epstein). "What is most Dickensian about him is his extraordinary combination of inwardness and expansiveness" (Jonathan Yardley). "Dickens's compassion was considerable. He sees duality in people; sometimes it's evil and comic, sometimes it's tender and comic" (Miriam Margolyes).

It's in his "Dickens: The Two Scrooges" (1940), "unquestionably the most influential single study of Dickens of the 20th century," that Edmund Wilson, "taking his title from the two manifestations of [Scrooge] of *A Christmas Carol,* the melancholy misanthrope and the joyful embodiment of Christmas cheer, [divided Dickens's own work—and conflicting temperaments—into] the dark vision of the later fiction and the comic ebullience of the early works" *(Oxford Readers Companion to Dickens).* Or, as Wilson words his blunt, and lay-shrink analysis, Charles Dickens was "the victim of a manic-depressive cycle." At last, after all of the earlier mewling, namby-pamby critical curlicues . . . a Dickens for our post-Freudian life!

"In the late novels you see over and over the story of

men who are two people coexisting in the same body. Dickens is more and more attracted to writing about that kind of character because that's how he felt in his later years" (Phyllis Rose). "Since he had taken up with Ellen, his heroes had passed from the simple, good-natured likes of Nicholas Nickleby, Oliver Twist, and David Copperfield to men haunted by guilt, snobbery, or other often unpleasant impulses, and often leading secret or shameful lives" (Phyllis Rose and Daniel Pool).

But in this, he was at one with the overarcing Victorian zeitgeist. "Studies of nineteenth-century sexuality have focused on the dualities of the age: the cramped parlors, the frilled pants on the piano legs, the antimacassars, the Sunday afternoon prayers for servants, all were set against a steamy underworld of scarlet bordellos, a famous madam named Skittle, pornographic dens, and flagellation chambers"; and so, if we decide that *Our Mutual Friend* is in part a study of "the duality of identity," that "just about every character has a sidekick, double, accomplice, or 'front' who mirrors, masks, or reverses a secret self," we're obliged to notice as well that "this divided-self theme haunts the late Victorians, culminating in Robert Louis Stevenson's *Dr. Jekyll and Mr. Hyde*" (Epstein).

Pool includes the lives of three other Victorian writers in his assessment: "If one were to press the double-life analogy, one might note that Marian Evans wrote under a [different gender] pseudonym, Wilkie Collins actually maintained not one but two mistresses simultaneously, and Miss Braddon lived in a delicate social subterfuge with her 'husband,' concealing the fact that he was still married to an insane woman whom he could not divorce."

Dickens's time, or—any time? Once we admit that we

live in a universe born of flyaway energy; that the wars of Good and Evil for our souls—those gauzy trophies—are assumed by nearly all of the world's religions; that the microblips inside the whirl-and-jolt inside the atoms inside the cells of our bodies bubble from alpha to zed and back nonstop . . . well, then we're not surprised to turn away from a chapter of Dickens and find, under "Crime" in *Time* for July 31, 2000 . . . this, entitled "Two-Faced Woman": "She has no visible halo, but the stocky, uneducated Chinese woman is a saint to thousands . . . a veritable goddess, dispensing both mercy and fortune. To the U.S. government, however, Big Sister Ping is a bigtime crook who ran a global crime network of gangsters that specialized in the brutal trade in humans from China, netting her more than $40 million. For years, law enforcement called her the Mother of all Snakeheads."

She might just as well be in the "Science" section, demonstrating subparticles from a mysterious Planckian physics that are coevally ingots of gold and dots of sea foam; pigs of iron and whiffs of honeysuckle; lugs of cement and weightless, milky, baby's breath.

37

If, in a technical, penetrative sense, he *was* her lover. Even *that* remains a riddle Sherlock Holmes might beat his great brain-heavy forehead against without any result except an unsightly dent beneath the brim of his deerstalker hat.

"I cannot believe they didn't have sex. I cannot believe that he would leave a wife who physically revolted him to turn to an obsessive ideal that he didn't touch" (Phyllis Rose). There's even jotted mysteria in his daybook that would lead us to believe that Nelly gave birth to a child (dead soon after). Still, there isn't proof of this; and anyway, simple proof of the child wouldn't be proof that it was his.

Miriam Margolyes: "Michael Slater is the quintessential Dickens scholar, and he didn't think Dickens had slept with Nelly. Neither does Dickens's biographer Peter Ackroyd"—who argues that the relationship "acted for Dickens as the realisation of one of his most enduring fictional fantasies . . . sexless marriage to a young, idealised virgin."

Go know (translation: one never can), my mother used to say while giving a beautifully practiced cosmic shrug.

38

Dateline Spring 2001: "A survey conducted by Olay beauty cream reveals 18 percent of women admit to having lied about their age."

(Eliza: "Yeah? Well, men lie, too. Let me put it like this: I've swallowed their lies a couple of times.")

[And my wife adds: "All it means is that a lot of women are willing to lie *about* lying about their age."]

39

There's a series of detective novels by William J. Palmer in which the Sherlock Holmes role is filled by Dickens, his real-life friend the novelist Wilkie Collins serving as Watson-like narrator. In *The Highwayman and Mr. Dickens,* Collins says, "Strange that both Dickens and I were so hopelessly captivated by actresses. I am convinced now that it was the uncertainty of them. . . . His beloved Ellen and my Meggy exhibited protean powers, that slippery ability to change shape and elude one's grasp."

40

She was on the floor—humming, on her back. She often thought best this way. She often communed with her charges best this way—her charges the stars. Her garden the size of the sky. She'd be up here in her office in the Observatory sometimes six days a week, long days that included the nights. Thinking. Humming. Smoking. Her favorite color of dress was orange, says her daughter, and her fingertips after an evening of concentration were tobacco orange to match. The stars were often scanned in tiger-lily oranges against their jet black field. Humming, thinking, sipping cocoa on the upper floor of Building D, and sometimes looking through the fifteen-incher under its great rotunda, which (although she knew the cosmos wasn't shaped to fit our human fancies) she'd imagine was the same curve that, in macrosize, provided a final border to everything knowable. *If* there was a border, and *if* everything was knowable. Maybe it wasn't. Still, she was making her contribution. She had faith in reason. (*Is* that oxymoronic? Anyway, it's what she had, and what she practiced.) Noting, thinking, even talking to the stars. "When I was a small child I used to ask to be told a story after being put to bed. Perhaps the supply of stories ran low, or the narrators wearied, and I was given to understand that the practice must cease. 'Very well,' said I, 'I will tell stories to myself.' And I did so, making them up as I went along." She hummed below the stars, she told them stories from childhood. Perhaps they told her stories, too—stories from *their* childhood, when energy wasn't matter yet, and the great heart of the universe was diffuse, and the first bonds waited.

⌒

She was born, with the century, in 1900: a solitary, studious, inquisitive girl from the start, a runner through meadows, noticer of grubs and constellations, stitcher of interesting connections among the world's odd jumble of things. Her parents were educated, encouraging. Step-great-aunt Dora "had been one of the early students at Newnham College and had been trained as a botanist." Aunt Florence was "a brilliant outspoken woman who became a professional pianist," knew peers of the realm, and considered Henry James "her most valued friend." It was both a privileged childhood, and one skewed from the normal paths in ways that make adolescence—and its need for friends—a difficult, uphill climb. "Trees were my earliest companions," and in a grove of maples at the bottom of their garden, she would while away a day with an invisible playmate, Grenson.

"One winter evening my mother was wheeling me in my pram, and we saw a brilliant meteorite blaze across the sky above Boddington Wood. She told me what it was, and taught me the right name for it by making a little rhyme: *As we were walking home that night / We saw a shining meteorite.* It was my first encounter with astronomy."

And: "I knew, had always known, that I wanted to be a scientist." By the time she was twelve, she was stealing up to the top floor of her schoolhouse, where a little room devoted to brief and simple lessons in science held a small range of bottles of chemicals. While everyone else was at church, Cecilia would "sit conducting a little worship service of my own, adoring the chemical elements—the stuff of the world."

A wondrous world; at times a cruel one, too. When she was thirteen and the family doctor reported "there was nothing to be done" about "a growth of facial hair"—"I burst into tears." Well, yeah: it must have seemed to her to be ruination, and the portent of a future written over by a scrawl of humiliation. "'Never mind, Cecilia,' he said kindly, 'you've got brains. Make something of them.' It was not much comfort, but it stiffened my resolve to become a scientist.

"So I sought an outlet in active scientific work."

∿

"I found a remarkable rose on the cliffs of Cornwall. . . ." Flowers, it was, at first. Shoots, shrubs, trees, bushes, mosses. Xylem and phloem. Soil and sap. And then in a moment—she called it "a thunderclap"—all of her dedication began to orbit a different nucleus.

In 1919—the same year in which Max Planck received the Nobel Prize for fathering quantum mechanics, and aspiring writer Ray Cummings published his science-fantasy novelette "The Girl in the Golden Atom"—Cecilia Payne received a ticket ("almost by accident": only four had been allotted to students at Newnham College, of which one fell in her keeping only because a friend of hers was "unable to go") to a lecture by Sir Arthur Stanley Eddington in the Great Hall of Trinity College.

He was recently back from an instruments-laden expedition to Príncipe Island, off the coast of western equatorial Africa; there, "among the mosquitoes and monkeys" (Leonard Shlain), Eddington photographed stars near the edge of the sun on May 29, the day of its total eclipse. His history-making, future-shaping results confirmed the general theory of relativity Einstein had introduced just a few years earlier. Space-time was pliable; space, *space itself*, could be bent like a bar of india rubber, and so could its light. This is what he announced to the packed-in scientific panjandrums. They came into the Hall, they took seats and straightened their ties, and an hour later they were sitting in a completely different universe than before—completely different, from the nebulae down to the air held out of shock and suspense in the bottom cup of their lungs.

For Cecilia Payne, "it was almost like a religious conversion" (Bartusiak). She says, "When I returned to my room I found that I could write down the lecture word for word. For three nights, I think I did not sleep. The experience was so acute, so personal, my world had been so shaken, that I experienced something very like a nervous breakdown. The upshot was, perhaps, a foregone conclusion."

Not long after, during a public night at Cambridge University, the shy but driven Cecilia Payne encouraged herself to approach her idol—"the greatest intellect" she had ever met, the man who first gave written words to the emerging scientific understanding of the "dishevelled atoms with only a few tatters left of their elaborate cloaks of electrons" at the heart of a star—and she said to him, out of a world that had, until then, been defined for her by plant life, and also out of a knowledge that women were unknown in (were *specifically prohibited* in places from admission to) observatory work . . . she said, "I should like to be an astronomer."

And he looked at her—he held her gaze for a long consideration; and did he look inside, to *her* atoms?— and Sir Arthur Stanley Eddington answered, "I can see no insuperable objection."

Then, from her autobiography: "He had opened the doors of the heavens to me."

∽

Even at the start, it was there. "It did not take me long to feel that I lived in a man's world. I felt from the first that my brother was the one who really mattered." ("Brilliant, warm-hearted," she adds of him, to be fair.) It was Humfert who got to ride in their godfather's "glorious" two-horse carriage ("In vain did I beg to be taken too"), and Humfert who was allowed on that occasion "to wear the coveted red gaiters that were a special mark of distinction. I watched them canter away, and it seemed like the end of the world." His exalted redness disappearing into the distance . . . a cranberry: bitter.

"Why," she asked her schoolteacher Lizzie Edwards, "was Jesus a man and not a woman?" And when her mother finally, *finally* answered "where babies come from": "What are men for, then?"

She grew up, from age four onward, in a fatherless household. Schooling was gender-segregated; even Newnham College (Cambridge) kept her from male company: "thus Cecilia apparently never met a young man as a casual friend or peer until she arrived [age twenty-three] in Massachusetts" (Virginia Trimble). (To Eliza's easily sexy sensibility, and to her generation's sense of casual sexual back-and-forth—of eros as osmosis—this would seem less like a mode of schoolhouse protocol, and more like balkanization.) Trimble goes on to describe Payne's being "tall and broad shouldered in an era that valued petiteness. Presumably she would have wished it otherwise. At some deep level, the young Cecilia Payne felt that she was not attractive." All in all, a recipe for high emotions, once a dollop of frustrated hormones is whisked immiscibly into the batter.

Given gender restrictions in England, her future on graduation would be "teaching at a girls' school"—little else was thinkable. But a friend "told me that a woman would have a better chance to be an astronomer in the United States," and in 1923 Cecilia Payne took leave of her native country and her family, for a new land "where there are no primroses, where the violets have no scent, where one will seek in vain for purple heather and golden gorse." The trade-off? "In Cambridge I had always been tired; the damp chill of the fenland air seemed to penetrate my bones. By contrast, the heady atmosphere of New England in October was so stimulating, nothing seemed impossible. Once I worked," she writes as if it's the Cinderella dream of every 23-year-old woman come true at last, "for 72 hours without sleep!"

∽

And it *was* an exhilarating time. She took notes on atomic structure in lectures by Niels Bohr himself, the mind who was responsible for classifying electron orbits. *Bohr himself!*—the cartographer of electrons!

On the audience end of his heavily accented speech,

she spent days writing down information on something called "soup groups"—only later, as she recounts with a smile, "emended to 'sub-groups.'"

◡

She was the only woman student who attended Ernest Rutherford's lectures—Rutherford, the man who first suggested the existence of an atomic nucleus; Rutherford, the "towering blond giant with a booming voice." At every lecture he'd gaze at her pointedly, there where she sat in the front row center, and start with "*Ladies* and Gentlemen." "All the boys regularly greeted this witticism with thunderous applause, stamping with their feet in the traditional manner, and at every lecture I wished I could sink into the earth."

Female, she was ineligible for academic appointments at not only all-male institutions, but many coeducational ones as well (Peggy A. Kidwell: "Even some women's colleges, such as Radcliffe, had no women on the faculty"). When she taught part of an introductory graduate course in astronomy at Harvard, she was paid indirectly under "equipment." When Harlow Shapley proposed that her course on variable stars be included, sensibly enough, in the Harvard course catalogue, "President Lowell and the Dean of the Faculty rejected this idea outright." Even more frustrating: telescope time, in an era when it was thought improper for women to spend a nightlong shift in the company of men. When Henry Norris Russell recommended Cecilia Payne for a new position opened at the Dominion Astrophysical Observatory in British Columbia—"quite the best of the young folks," said his nominating letter—the reply was "there would be difficulty about the observing end of it with a woman in this isolated place and I think we can hardly consider her."

Virginia Trimble: "A recent letter from my thesis advisor recalls an incident where a group of astronomers were discussing a suitable gift for C-P-G on some significant birthday, and the winner (at least on the laugh meter) was 'a shaving machine.' It is by no means the most unpleasant tale I heard in preparing for this introduction."

A chill night—chill and clear. Walking home down a leaf-skittered street, the snap of a Massachusetts fall in her nostrils, and the sequin-jointed bodies of gods and goddesses in the sky. Up there . . . a parity. Up there . . . world cultures honored their various Amazon and Hercules warriors equally. Just look at them, she thought. Those bodies composed of connected medallions.

In 1926 she became "the youngest astronomer ever starred in J. M. Cattell's *American Men of Science.*"

⌒

This is because in 1925 her Ph.D. thesis (the book that's also known as Harvard monograph number 1, *Stellar Atmospheres)* was "undoubtedly the most brilliant Ph.D. thesis ever written in astronomy" (Struve and Zebergs, 1962). Jesse L. Greenstein, in 1982: "What it contains is part of our daily heritage as scientists. She read everything applicable and, long before the atomic data were available or reliable, she used (or even corrected) all that she read. A rich memory, an eye for detail, are accompanied by bravery in applying the then new physics to the stars." In a magical statement, Trimble says that the thesis "answered the very basic question of what stars are made of." As a result of that inquiry, "modern historians of science (e.g., Hufbauer, 1991) firmly credit her with the discovery that most things in the universe are made mostly of hydrogen." (It's easy to see how this infinite uniformity called to the diced-apart life Eliza knew, with an urgent appeal.)

Also, she was a member of the American Astronomical Society; and the International Astronomical Union; and the American Academy of Arts and Sciences; and the Royal Astronomical Society; and was elected to the American Philosophical Society.

And she received the Radcliffe College Award of Merit; and the Rittenhouse Medal of the Franklin Institute; and the Henry Norris Russell Prize of the American Astronomical Society; and five honorary doctorates from institutions wanting the secondhand glow of her own incandescence.

And in 1956 she became Chairman of Harvard's Department of Astronomy and, in consequence, a full professor—"the first woman at Harvard promoted to this rank."

And she authored eight major books on astronomical subjects, and a booklength autobiography, plus she authored (or co-authored)—I've counted them, as duly as she tracked the thin spectroscopy lines of solar radiation—341 papers/articles . . .

. . . this woman born of the sad girl watching her brother Humfert *(humf!)* ride off in a solo ball of red glory.

Most things in the universe are made mostly of hydrogen. . . . This, then, is the amniotic tissue that nurtured the structuring of the cosmos, and nurtures it still.

This woman some nights on the floor of her office,

resting after labor, and curled in the fetal position, and humming, and almost floating in an ocean of stars.

⌢

"To my husband, 'that bright particular star'"—the dedication line (with assistance from Shakespeare) of her final book.

She and Sergei Gaposchkin met in Germany, at a convening of the Astronomische Gesselschaft. "He was one who had resolved, as I had resolved, to be an astronomer—and against what terrible odds!"—by which she means the political climate in Soviet Russia. "Of course I knew I must help him to escape. I had never tried to exert any influence before, but I tried it now. A place was found at Harvard. . . ."

Seemingly, in her heart as well. "It led to the uniting of two lives, the flowing of two rivers, bound for the same goal, into one channel." They married in March of 1934.

In his own recollections, Gaposchkin says Cecilia was "like a ripe peach left alone on the tree, darkened, wrinkled a little outside, but the more delicious inside"—a strange, slant compliment. Sexually, she was "totally inexperienced." Their daughter says that they "loved each other intensely at first"; those last two words seem pointedly frosty. "There were professional disagreements" . . . "he behaved flamboyantly," she was a "stoic" . . . "the problems of bringing up a family on a very limited income must have been large" . . . but "in truth they loved each other deeply" she says, attempting to rub some circulation into the frostbit areas.

A limited income . . . yes, and she tells the story of when "my mother purchased a surplus parachute; its yards and yards of uncontrollable gossamer white nylon were turned into practical underthings."

So—is she wearing a pair of those frugally scissored "step-ins" under her bright-as-a-toucan orange dress? I'd like to think so. On her office floor in Cambridge, Massachusetts, with her sex held by the touch of a cloth intended to float through the sky. There's something right about that, as she cradles her knees, as she thinks of going over for a night's stay at the telescope. The sky: it couldn't have been, no *person* could have been, more intimate with her than this imagined touch of ours.

When she was six, in school, she learned to recite *The Pied Piper of Hamelin* by heart. She's at the telescope now; and it isn't a flute, but it is in a way: a great flute for the music of the spheres. And the stars are following her, are in a line and marching, are enthralled by the tune that she plays for them.

41

It's then that I notice, *really notice,* something—and I get a glimmer of understanding. (I'll tell you about it later.)

42

Although Darrell Standing, *The Star Rover's* narrator, undertakes a number of disembodied journeys backward into earlier selves in earlier moments of history, he also describes his failed attempt at alleviating solitary confinement through imagined games of chess: "Exercise it was, for there could be no real contest when the same player played both sides. I tried, and tried vainly, to split my personality into two personalities. . . . But ever I remained the one player."

43

Pepys: "I know nothing that can give a better notion of infinity and eternity than being upon the sea in a little vessel without anything in sight but yourself."

44

She read Shakespeare. She also attended serious theater with a passionate devotion. ("She once remarked to me, in a discussion of careers, that if she had not become a scientist she would probably have become an actress, clearly not a Hollywood-style actress, but an English stage actress.") And when, in her teens, she taught a Sunday school class of "slum children, very likely from illiterate homes," she brought in her brother and sister for a production of *Hamlet* "in which I doubled as Gertrude and Horatio."

I imagine nights in the Observatory that *weren't* alone: she'd speak the lines of the Bard aloud to her close friends at the other end of the telescope.

She knew not only Shakespeare by heart, but swatches of Lewis Carroll. Precocity claimed her. "When I was about 13 I began to write verse. I betook myself to the sonnet, the vilanelle, the rondel, the rondeau redoublé. I was not modest in my undertakings. I projected a didactic poem in rhymed Alexandrines that was to cover all the sciences in 10 cantos." She could write "backwards, upside-down, and upside-down-backwards." As Peggy Kidwell says, "I listened to a course of hers in variable stars, and what I learned was the English language."

She was fluent in French and German. She read Russian, Latin, ancient Greek, Italian (one of her favorites: Dante). "Icelandic was a minor challenge." Her daughter says "she was also an inspired cook, a marvelous seamstress, and inventive knitter," and pegs to this "experi-

ments with woodworking, bookbinding, cardplaying";
one old friend addends "construction of mechanical toys
from cardboard and cotton." (She remembered her father
would visit the children's nursery with his handmade
wooden bricks, and lead them in planning out "minia-
ture Stonehenges.")

Either alone (at first) or later with her family, she traveled the world. An immigrant herself, who wed an immigrant she'd helped in immigrating, Payne-Gaposchkin
held an especially knowing tenderness for the displaced.
She and Sergei founded Harvard's Forum for International Problems; targeted in the 1950s as "dangerous" by
HUAC standards, Sergei was called to testify by a government panel of busybody McCarthyites—*very* unpleasant.

Her interest in botany goes back to the point where
her memory starts: her autobiography opens when,
"about eight years," she recognizes a certain flower—
"bee orchis"—on her own, and "I think my life as a scientist began at that moment." At age twelve, she was
reading, "with the aid of a dictionary, an old treatise
using the Linnaean System of classification, with text in
German and French." She made an herbarium. She won
"a coveted prize" at school and asked, as her reward, for
"a textbook on fungi." At age nineteen, she was busy
"transcribing Scott's *Fossil botany* into a notebook." Were
there boys? Were there ribbons she bought for her hair? "I
found a fascinating group of desmids among the more
humdrum algae."

Now do we see her completely? No. She was also that
heavy, heartsore girl who cried herself to sleep because of
facial hair the local physician said was beyond his ability; the mother who pinned the wash to the line (all her
life, she refused an electric dryer); the source for the name

of "the minor planet 1974 CA, discovered at Harvard Observatory's Agassiz Station, and designated 'Payne-Gaposchkin' in her honor." *Now?* No; not now; there are too many pieces. Still, we can *try* to walk around the mountain's base (*montagne,* Montaigne: who said "I find in myself such infinite depth and variety, that what I have learned bears no fruit other than this—to make me realize how much I have yet to learn").

This woman adding her stars to an album of stars, as once, in a bed of a far-off land, when she should have been sleeping, she lit a candle and set, in an album of cheap, rough paper, her morning's collection of ferns and meaty petals and great light-guzzling leaves.

She played the violin (Saint Cecilia is patroness of musicians). "My father began my musical education when I was two weeks old." At eight, an Albert Hall performance of the *Messiah* swept her to tears. As a student at Cambridge, she conducted an award-winning choir. She founded the Observatory Philharmonic Orchestra and conducted its premier concert. She hummed. She scanned the sky all night and kept the stars from falling asleep by serenading them with *The British Grenadiers* and *The Galway Piper.* They may have sung back to her in return. And when the cancer had finally made a lacy interior shroud of her lungs . . . when she could no longer speak . . . her children "brought music, the *Messiah* and Mozart's *The Magic Flute.* A beatific look came across her face as the first strains of that soft music reached her ears from the tiny speaker placed on her pillow. The following morning she died in her sleep.

"She gave her body to science."

45

Cecilia Payne-Gaposchkin addresses the woo of the older physics, in describing a certain way of approaching botany: " . . . the panorama of the plant world, so neatly classified, so convincingly understood in terms of Natural Selection." This is the science of filling in empty drawers of a pre-labeled wall of drawers. This is a filing system, under our control and at our service, and its comforts are many.

The filing cabinets, though, are in an office; and the office has a door. On the other side of that door is a world that won't be alphabetized for the sake of the files. That world might even say there *aren't* cabinets, there *isn't* a door, there's only flux in shaped electrostasis. And then . . . ? "I saw before me a science which seemed to be utterly unreal," she says. [For example,] "The outer structure of the atom and of the atomic nucleus are elusive. But the understanding of unexplained phenomena is, and ought to be, the goal of every scientist."

She was willing to walk through the door. She was willing to walk through the "door."

⌒

In 1919—the year in which Ray Cummings published "The Girl in the Golden Atom," and Eddington voyaged down to Africa to conduct the observations that in essence validated Einstein's theory of relativity—Max Planck was awarded the Nobel Prize for fathering the field of quantum physics. Even at the start, it was a sanity unraveler. Planck had redefined the universe as "two-tracked." This is why, to quote an issue of *Discover,* "an ocean of particles continuously pops into and out of existence all around us." When they're "out of existence," what they really are is "in existence" in the other track—or call it another universe.

Ah, our conscious-subconcious, testosterone-estrogen, credulous-doubtful, birth-death, sad and lovely bifurcated lives!

What we now suspect, 101 years after Planck's revealing of quantum mechanics, is that there may be many tracks, much more than two, may even be infinite tracks—or call it infinite ("parallel"? "congruent"? do we need a new term altogether?) universes. *Discover* says: "The laws of quantum theory insist that the fundamental constituents of reality, such as protons, electrons, and other subatomic particles, are not hard and indivisible. They behave like both waves and particles. They can appear out of pure void, and disappear. A single particle occupies not just one position but exists here, there, and many places in between. *See footnote 34, last sentence.*

"Physicist David Deutsch argues that the theory's laws must hold true at every level of reality. Because everything in the world, including ourselves, is made of these particles, and because quantum theory has proved infallible in every conceivable experiment, the same weird quantum rules must apply to us.

"We, too, must exist in many states at once, even if we don't realize it"—so all of us have twin counterparts in an überconstruct of (maybe) infinite universes. This isn't Ray Cummings's socko-smasho-smoocho story anymore: this is serious science. This is the ocean, once we've walked the Planck.

⌢

Is that what dreams, or some dreams, are—a leak, a scent, let out of a sibling universe? Is that what prophecy is, or intuition? Does this explain the occult, or only raddle its weave incomprehensibly?

In Cranston, Rhode Island, in 1991, "a 7-year-old girl whose Siamese twin sister died, and who realized her own death was minutes away, discussed her last wishes with her parents." These were a list of friends to give flowers to, and an expressed desire to be cremated "because she didn't want to be in a box," said her mother, "she wanted to be free."

The newspaper coverage says, "Their favorite activity was biking on a custom two-seat tricycle that let one girl pedal and the other relax"—one in, one out, of their relative states. As if they provide us a human-level hint of the greater cosmos.

⌢

On an island of the Encantadas that used to shelter "for months at a time" the vilest stripe of pirate, Melville discovers "old ruins of what had once been symmetric lounges of stone and turf—seats which might have served Brahmins and presidents of peace societies—undoubtedly, made by the Buccaneers.

"I cannot avoid the thought, that it is hard to compute the construction of these romantic seats to any other motive than one of pure peacefulness and kindly fellowship with nature. That the Buccaneers perpetrated the greatest outrages is very true—that some of them were mere cut-throats cannot be denied. Could it be possible, that they robbed and murdered one day, revelled the next, and rested themselves by turning meditative philosophers on the third?

"Not very improbable, after all. For consider the vacillations of a man."

Consider the columns of doubleness in *everyone*— although it will be an individual doubleness for each.

Cecilia Payne-Gaposchkin: "When I was four years old, my father died suddenly. For the rest of my childhood I felt I was not like other children, for I had *two* fathers in heaven."

46

"*She* read Shakespeare: I read Shakespeare" . . . either then or later, would Eliza have thought of Hamlet's words?—"This most excellent canopy, the air, look you, this brave o'erhanging firmament, this majestical roof fretted with golden fire—why, it appeareth nothing to me but a foul and pestilent congregation of vapours."

47

And the mold—the baseline human mold—is sometimes broken more literally:

Of a not atypical shaman initiation, as reported by the participant: *The god-wolves came, they took off my head with a hatchet, they set it onto a tree stump. So now I could watch. They tore off my arms, they tore off my legs, they scattered these in the directions of snow, of sun, of the plants, of the animals. They tore out my heart and ate it, then they danced, they drank my blood, and then they vomited out a new heart. Now my legs ran back, my arms flew back like birds, and then they reattached my head. So now I was whole again, and my eyes could see to see how to heal my people.*

This is pancultural global wisdom, which maybe the women on the calendar of mastectomy survivors have: "eyes [that] see to see" there *is* a next life. Yes, but first the old one needs to be dismembered.

༄

Of the amputees of heroic coping . . . Cecilia Payne-Gaposchkin reminisces about astronomer L. J. Comrie: "Crippled and deafened by war wounds, he was still extremely active and played a formidable game of tennis in spite of having lost a leg."

༄

Not that this rules out more comedic examples. Of these, I choose the man at Incredible's Lounge in El Paso,

Texas, who, both drunk and angry, whipped out a gun. . . . "He never got to point it at anyone, though. That's when his artificial arm fell off."

Mr. Stupid, yes. But I also give him my annual Gumption Award.

48

"The whole place was crawling with maggots," Stacy Chaffey said, in another story of muckily unsanitary retrieval . . . in this instance, of her $20,000 engagement ring that fiancé Sal Licata had accidentally thrown into the trash. Next day, they raced to the neighborhood landfill, where he waded "into a foul-smelling mound of rubbish 4 feet deep, 12 feet across, and 100 feet long." It took him nearly four hours—and even that was miraculous—before he could victoriously lift those carats up to the sun that shines its light on alabaster shrines and garbage dumps alike.

49

Three men are in a private room at their club. They've been there in shifts for forty continuous hours. Outside: Manhattan, all of its engine-throb and bands of night-time bijoux-twinkle. Also outside: the War—the War to End All Wars—since this is the twentieth century in its difficult torn-apart teens.

But neither the costly battle for democracy, nor the avenues of lithesomely arrayed lights that, in wartime even, can't completely mute their very American sense of mink-and-greasepaint gaiety . . . neither of these hemispheres of New York's sensibility exerts any sort of gravitic pull on the atmosphere of this one room, or dissipates the charge of its expectancy, or rushes the gray-blue wreaths of its cigar smoke from their floating promenade—like lush lifesavers—in the thick air near the ceiling.

"Come here, quick, I see something." A quarter of three in the A.M.

"Where?"

"There by the scratch; he's sprawled there; I can see him."

—The scratch that once had been a canyon.

And the Doctor, the Big Business Man, and the Very Young Man begin to attend to their pinpoint ward, who's "growing perceptibly larger with each instant"—soon, who's "sitting sidewise on the ring" as if it's a coliseum wall-top; then, who's sizeable enough for a revivifying brandy.

"Well, gentlemen, I suppose that you are interested to hear what happened to me." They've had their dinner by now, and over port and cigars are ready for the saga of his expansion, through the subvoid, to the "true" world of their friendly sight . . . that is, to "the blue sky overhead that I knew was the space of this room."

The lesson: It isn't only that a lost ring can return to a man.

A lost man can return from a ring.

⌣

And the gold and sapphire ring that Katie Smith and Dave Gould lost as they packed up for a 4-month trip of 10,000 miles, from Yorkshire to Egypt, the U.S.A., and Costa Rica, journeying through the jungle, climbing mountain terrain . . . *that* ring? "Before flying home, Mr. Gould cleaned the mud-caked boots he had been wearing almost continuously—and discovered the ring jammed into one boot's tread."

If we'll only look through eyes that have been sensitized to seeing wholes instead of fractions, acts of recompletion are the infrastructure circles onto which our lives get architected.

The *Times* reports a fisherman who lost his keys in Loch Broom: six weeks later, one hundred miles away, while he was sailing off the island of Rassay, they were vomited up by a large cod. Ricky Shipman of Sunset Beach, California—his drivers license—eleven years later: a mackerel. Of wonders, signs, and portents such as these, there is no limit in the annals of miraculous return.

And, as I've said, the cats and dogs. The "well-bred collie" in Edwin Arnold's book *The Soul of the Beast* was shipped by its master (who lived in the port town of Inverkeithing, Scotland) to a friend (in Calcutta, India). It arrived, but shortly disappeared—and a few months later, "out of the blue," was suddenly wagging its tail at the door of its old Inverkeithing address ("evidently it had stowed away at Calcutta on a ship bound for Dundee"). A similar story from the *Sunday Express* reports a mere forty-eight miles of forth and back; but it's a *hedgehog*. Of these two-way trips that stun our biped reasoning, a full encyclopedia of stats could be compiled. Even "ordinary" migratory loops of certain birds provide us with a measurement for "closure" that spans continents. What orrery, what star show in those teacup skulls, positions them in flightspace with precision of a kind our cockpit crews can only dream of?

And the five-pound note with which Mark Goldsmith paid for his petrol in Cheltenham, Gloucestershire: two weeks later and two hundred miles away, he received it back in his change at a grocery store (it bore a pair of glasses and a mustache on the Queen, thanks to his six-year-old Picasso-of-a-daughter, Clare). And remains of a village buried during storms in 1606, St.-Ismail's, "surfaced again when the dunes were swept away by winter storms." And five wild choughs were seen this year in Cornwall, "thirty years after the last of these birds were known to be native to England." And a small black terrier cross, named Sweetie, was hit by a truck in Wentzville, Missouri, and, in the absence of a discernible heartbeat, duly buried by owner Glenda Stevens: a few hours later, Sweetie "was very boisterously digging herself from out of her grave." Of everyday saints and everyday holy sites, the bedside bibles of return are filled to a richness matched by only the everynight stars that wheel unde-terred through the heavens on their great black disc, and also disappear, and also come back to us.

When Ahab and his crew go down, the shipping firm considers it a loss; and the families left behind tear at their own skin, in grief at this loss; and the novel's reader shares in this, as the surface calms, and the sky clamps down like a coffin lid over this loss.

But to the ocean—to the deep holds of the first cells—it's a homecoming.

⌣

If we'll only look through eyes that have been sensitized to see-ing wholes instead of fractions . . . what then? To the vision of the background radiation from the universe's birth; to the understanding of a rock, or its cousin the moon, or the tribes of all of the moons; to the point of view of the seraphim riding on fiery sunset clouds like herds of horses; to the consciousness, if "consciousness" comes close at all, of the fire and of the clouds . . . to these, there might be only one thing here, if "thing" and "here" come close at all, there might be a Totality and only a Totality, and every amputated arm, lost penny, and divided per-sonality would have its own place in a cosmogestalt that, itself, is beyond being broken. This may be what the physicists call the Grand Unified Theory. Some might call it God. To the ocean, it might simply be What Is—the ocean's only possible thought, if "thought" comes close at all. To the time kept by the inside of the ocean, Ahab may come down to the sea bed like a bolt of light-ning, uniting (as lightning always does) the upper and the lower planes. This is cohesion—natal, fatal, and resurrectory at once—of the kind suggested in these lines from a poem by the painter Albert Pinkham Ryder:

> . . . mingling shadows
> Into deeper shadows
> Of sky and land reflected.

∽

Eyes that have been sensitized to seeing wholes. . . . It must have felt that way to the Romantic-era poets and their scientist peers: a symbiosis. Shelley conducted gassy, frizzling, eggy chemical experiments (historian Paul Johnson says, "His *Witch of Atlas,* with energy supplied by electricity and magnetism, is the earliest great poem of space travel"); and Mary Shelley knew enough about the serious eighteenth- and nineteenth-century biology lab to dream such research into her grand, albeit cautionary, *Frankenstein.* Wordsworth says the poet "will be ready to follow the steps of the man of science. . . . He will be at his side, carrying sensation into the midst of the objects of the science itself. The remotest discoveries of the chemist, the botanist, or mineralogist will be as proper objects of the poet's art as any."

Coleridge worked with Humphry Davy (who was "already regarded as Britain's leading scientist") in early protophotography attempts to fix an image. They exchanged a correspondence on the effect of nitrous oxide (Coleridge: "I could not avoid . . . beating the ground with my feet; and after the mouth-piece was removed, I remained for a few seconds motionless, in great extacy"). Robert Southey and Peter Roget (of *Thesaurus* fame) were part of this company; floating in nitrous oxide, they experienced the wholeness of existence, felt its disparate elements surge together to make a Singularity, an All . . . *the infrastructure circles onto which our lives get architected.*

Or, as a character says in Clifford D. Simak's *Shakespeare's Planet:* "As if someone had taken you to some great cosmic mountaintop, with the universe all spread out before you—all of the glory and the wonder, all the sadness. All the love and hate, all the compassion and not-caring."

Darrell Standing in *The Star Rover,* as he reports on one of his exo-corporeal forays: "I was bound on vast adventure, where, at the end, I would find all the cosmic formulae and have made clear to me the ultimate secret of the universe."

In *What Painting Is,* his highly original study of painting in terms of classical alchemy, art historian James Elkins tells us, "*Gur* is the substance that congeals into anything: it is equally fitted, as the author [an anonymous 'traditional alchemist'] puts it, 'for the information of an ass, or an ox, or for any metal.'"

Congeals into anything . . . the hand-of-hands that shadows the wall with titmouse, Viking-helmeted opera soloist, condor, astronaut, street pimp, stegosaurus, nurse's assistant, circus clown, Ebola virus, Elvis impersonator and Elvis-prime . . . as if we're all there, you and me and Eliza, Fanny Burney, the Ran-man, Shelley, *everybody,* held in the potential of absolute gur-ness, while the ocean reconfigurates the Pequod, and the lives of saints and dragons are retold in the stars, and atoms of bone are alchemized into atoms of soil and dew and rind, and the mind lays down in the universe, and the universe in the mind.

50

"What do you think?"

"Well . . . I'm of two minds."

Experts in the United States and Germany are claiming (this is according to German science journal *Geo*) a new, surprising literality for that wheezing cliché: they say they've discovered a knot of around 100 billion brain nerve cells (more than are held in the spinal cord) in the human stomach, and that this "second brain" may be the source "of unconscious decisions that the main brain later presents as a conscious decision of its own.

"'We now believe that there is a lot more to "gut feelings" than was previously believed,' says Professor Wolfgang Prinz, of [and this—along with the name "Prince of the Gang of Wolves"—is what pleases me, this is *so* sweet, this is what I'm sure would please the "two-track" master of physics himself] the Max Planck Institute for Psychological Research in Munich."

Afterword

And in a week it was September 11, 2001, and our milk-weed puffs of personal concern were lost inside the holocaustal winds of that unthinkable morning . . . And even knowing that—still, nothing ever stops everything from happening . . . A woman still waits at her phone for a message, tiny individual kabuki dramas of passion and redemption and betrayal and transcendence, of survival and grandiosity and jealousy, still play out on their stages in our minds and moods—those stages where the characters and the audience are one . . . The world is stained by terror, shaken with a new sense of fragility—and still, every morning we wake, and we're the embryo of that day . . . And at the end of every minute that's completed, we're the embryo of the minute that follows . . . The world is caught in horrible uncertainty, we know the atoms cooking in the farthest stars but still can't know if the building we enter will tumble or stand, we can't guess planes, we can't guess the safety of packages, we walk beneath the thought of those 3,000-plus who died, who incinerated to ozone—and still, a woman impatiently waits word on her biopsy, so selfish a concern in the martial air, in the sea of patriotism, and still she waits for the lab report, as if, to use the old cliché, as if her life depends on it . . . And still, out of habit she seizes upon the old motifs that shaped her life, she plucks them out of the media inundation of streaming info-facts, she shapes that chaos according to the themes by which she's lived—as one example, in the hellish rubble-clearance taking place around Ground Zero of the World Trade Center a few days in the wake of the 11th, "a pair of bound and severed hands was found" . . . If you pattern your world by seeing amputations, amputations is indeed what you will see . . . If your unit of measurement for the tenor of life is mystery body parts, you'll notice—tucked inside the overwhelming coverage of the bombing and the grieving and the anthrax—a report on the "86 human skulls discovered at a bus stop in Siliguri, north of Calcutta; and, 6 weeks later, 500 more in a house in Calcutta itself. Police investigating say they may have been collected for Tantric rites." . . . "A wife sawed off her husband's hand as he lay asleep after drinking." (Delhi) . . . "Fourteen churches at one time all claimed ownership of Jesus's foreskin." . . . Yes, but if the overriding metaphor by which you shape your life is one of reinstatement, *then* the great relentlessness of FBI alerts and shots of battle-smoke is leavened by the story of William McColgan, who lost his gold class ring (ten carats: St. John's High School in Shrewsbury, Mass.) in the waters of Cape Cod during the summer of 1971, and thirty years later had it returned by a David Taylor—who, on vacation at Cape Cod (from Missouri), was playing around onshore with his metal detector and heard a pinging from ten feet down: "It was totally black and covered with crusty underwater stuff." . . . As well as (speaking of fantastical return) Chamlong Taengnium, fifty-one, who said that the five-foot monitor lizard which followed her home from her thirteen-year-old son's cremation *was* her reincarnated son, it slept on his mattress, loved his favorite yoghurt drink, and brought good fortune: "Crowds of up to 200 people thronged to her house in Nonthaburi,

20 miles north of Bangkok, bringing the lizard gifts and inspecting its skin for lucky lottery numbers." . . . Items buried under the press of weightier news—"a terrorist threat to America's bridges," "fresh civilian casualties"— the way that an engagement ring or a scribbled prescription for antidepressant is buried below the ashy slag of the New York devastation . . . If a woman keeps her TV on, she can follow the international upheavals and still attend to her phone, which is on, is silent now but filled with enormously loud potential . . . If this woman is Eliza, it's not a cell phone, no, it's a wall-mount model ("I want my conversation to be *stable,* dammit, not jittering all over town on a thousand errands") . . . If you're a crazy sonofabitch, a real scumbag, then your errand today is hunkering unobtrusively in the shadows as the membership of AGED WELL (Amity General Emeritus Doctors' Weekend Educational Lecture series on Longevity) leaves the building for the parking lot: that asshole fuck physician who thinks he's too good to shit like the rest of us, he's had an affair with this man's wife, the cheating cunt, and now he's got to learn that there's a price tag on adultery . . . And the crazy sonofabitch stands patting the gun in his holster with what looks like marsupial affection . . . This all keeps happening, the parfait, stew bone, olla podidra, confetti-strewn, ragtag, haggis-and-ragout simultaneity-universe keeps happening in its every hair, in each impeccably engineered joint of a cheese mite: while the President is issuing another national "vigilance watch" and the Secretary of This and the Advisor of That are grimly circling questions the size of aircraft carriers, everyday concerns the size of cysts won't be denied their rooted hold on our attention . . .

It's the way that, as your fascinated stare attempts to comprehend the monolithic bulk of Moby-Dick, that coliseum of flesh, that moon of muscle and oil: still, in its shadow, still, on the fringes of things, the epics of the plankton are sung, and the ecosystem inhabited by the gill-worm is as actual as any . . . And speaking of Moby-Dick: and speaking of the whale's ecosystem-partner, Ahab: what to make of Chris Moon, "one leg and one arm" after volunteering to help a charity clear land mines in Cambodia—who, by using "an artificial leg with a special flexible foot," completed (in "53 hours, 47 minutes and 7 seconds") the Badwater Ultra Marathon, "135 miles through Death Valley, where the desert heat reaches 130 degrees." . . . Do you remember the story that spritzled up into the gossipy air of the 1940s, something like a famous home-run hitter with a five-year-old daughter who'd lost a leg in a bad head-on collision, and an artificial one was artfully fashioned out of Humdinger One, his favorite (and now retired) bat . . . And speaking of artificial parts of the body: of more than 50,000 mastectomy patients who opt for reconstruction, 17 percent go on to get "additional surgery, trying to see that the natural one will 'match' its new and more erect and maybe larger partner." . . . And speaking of vision-yanking false fronts in that frequently eroticized region: Lori Barghini and friend were first inspired during a visit to Las Vegas: "There were a lot of beautiful women there, and we were like, 'How do we get guys' attention?' So my girlfriend puts caps from the little hotel shampoo bottles in her bra. All weekend long, everyone was happy to see us, we didn't have to wait in lines and we always got into the VIP section. I knew we were on to something," and they're now co-owners of Bodyperks, makers of prosthetic nipples: "Guys go gaga, and women have been calling shops desperate to find where to get them."—("a beautiful fake, like a planetarium ceiling" [William Matthews]) . . . Plus, from the Reuters news service, June 2, 2001, a report that police in Bogota, Colombia, arrested three women who "preyed on men" by luring them to lick their drug-smeared nipples: "Their victims promptly lost all will power, not to mention their wallets and cars." . . . But surely any men who acquiesced to that suspicious offer are themselves suspect, in many ways, of many unsavory possibilities: Louis Menand, in an essay on duplicity, says: "There is a tendency, when we think about lying in the abstract, to imagine the liar as a person operating in a world of innocents. But in real life there is not the lie on one side and everything that is not a lie on the other. The dissembler is always part of a universe of dissemblers. [A kind of moral "ecosystem," to retrieve a term I used a few sentences back.] This is not because everyone is dishonest; it is because all adult interactions take for granted a certain degree of insincerity and indirection. [A kind of moral quantum mechanics, in which the state of a given energy, the location of a subparticle, is (n)either here (n)or there.] There is always a literal meaning, which no one takes completely seriously, and an implied meaning, which is what we respond to even when we pretend to be responding to the literal meaning. Language comes shrouded in an assumptive fog." . . . And speaking of fog, of shroud: that woman on September 11, the one who videocammed the cloud of death, the cloud of 3,000 vaporized screams, a volcanic and *fleshy* cloud as it roamed the streets with the physical threatening presence

of a gang of goon marauders: she was pulled to safety
into a local storefront by a stranger, with only seconds to
spare, and through the window that faced the street kept
videoing the horror as it passed ("Oh God," "Oh God,"
"Oh God," a chorus in the background) slowly, sauntering, with all of the time in the world, like ink through
water, only this was death, oh this was people and architecture milled together as finely as the laws of the thermo-
chemical process allow, and no matter *what* physics says
about the ethereal properties of the quantum world, no
matter *what* the writings of Bohr would say about the in-
effable and invisible infra-elements that zip through us
unnoticed: on the human level at which our lives have
skin that lifts in prickles, science says that a mix like this
of asbestos and bone, of fire and tongues, will stick in our
dreams and keep us waking sweating in sudden startled
night-jolts for the rest (whatever that means) of our
days . . . Nothing ever stops everything from happening:
in 1919, as Niels Bohr was creating a language for quantum mechanics, and former Edison junior writer Ray
Cummings was creating the passionate world of the
golden atom, peace was hammered out—the Treaty of
Versailles—and the War to End All Wars came down to a
set of plenipotentiary signatures on a document page . . .
"Terrorists" and "cancer"—the unit of measurement
they have in common is "cells"—as if, in a universe
understood by Bohr and his progeny, they might be alternate states of the same one fear . . . So many abstrac-
tions to learn, and still, a woman is at her phone, a lab
report is in a stack of lab reports, another woman (C., who
has a cell phone, and has just arrived in Memphis for a
conference, despite her post-11th heebie-jeebies over fly-

ing) considers making a call to Eliza to say that she arrived okay—these are parts of the ongoing day, no less so than the World Trade Center dunes of wreckage sifted through on "real time" TV; and to the neutral hunger running through the universe, the small teakettle shrill with which this book began (in sentence six), may be a datum just as necessary as the gunshot that's about to take place soon . . . As neuroscientist Laura Otis says, "There is nothing more beautiful than a highly branched neuron waiting for inputs." . . . Is *that* what we are to the cosmos?—"inputs"? . . . *Is* a gun about to go off?—if so, will it connect? or miss? . . . I don't know, that's beyond the scope of this "Afterword," but I do know that a man in the evening murk outside of the Amity General Annex Auditorium is aiming at his target's head—or is that Jake's?—they look so much alike—is snugging the trigger, is teasing the trigger by touching it lighter than dew, is teasing it more delicately than he ever could a woman . . . And a woman, *his* woman for what it's worth and it's not worth a grasshopper's spit-up, is pacing—yes, again: from pool of light to pool of light, through shadows as drowningly deep as Victorian lampblack: pacing, worrying ulcered lining into her colon, knowing he's out there somewhere with idiot macho jealousy and an itchy gun: from a fifth-floor window, her life is as long as it takes to cross one pool of light—a mayfly life—and then she disappears off the map, to be reborn in the next of those visible circles . . . Her life, your life, everybody's: the notion, when it comes to us, that *everyone's* existence is as richly convoluted as one's own—or, as Julio Cortázar puts it, "eighty worlds and within each one eighty more, and within each of these: stupidities, coffee, information." . . . Coffee, that's what C. is thinking, weary and unpacking and fitting her clothes to the funny little motel-room hangers. . . . Where is Vern these days?—"motel" so often brings him back to mind . . . Is my former student the ambulance tech on duty tonight? . . . How many lives are involved in the sound of a distant siren? . . . Should I call Eliza, to see how she's doing? . . . How often we're hit from "out of the blue," as if the sky that Payne-Gaposchkin studied, studies us right back: "A servant girl struck by lightning at her bedside with a rosary in her hand, the beads being metal" (Melville) . . . Heads of state, and heads of terrorist cells, and talking news heads—do they sleep like any other human heads, what dreams get played upon the domes inside those skulls? . . . It's night; not quite "the dead of night," but night . . . Eliza waiting, toying with the gold ring on her finger . . . As Eric Browning says, in his article on the Legion of Super-Heroes, "Space precludes referencing all key stories here, especially the clashes with Computo, the Dark Circle, Universo and the Time Trapper." . . . Well, who *doesn't* trap time? . . . She thinks back to a child-her, petulant and whining *Whyyyyy* . . . The phone rings. She clutches her hand to her breast.

Acknowledgments

⌣

In quoting others we cite ourselves.

—JULIO CORTÁZAR

What would a kaleidoscope be without its constituent bits of arrangeable wonder? *Pieces of Payne* is built around the following sources. Many, I've rummaged deeply and relied upon most heavily. Others, I more or less superstitiously kept nearby like lucky touchstones. All receive my gratitude.

Some people and publications mentioned in the main text aren't to be found in this list of acknowledgments. As with, for example, Peter Ackroyd and Miriam Margolyes and Phyllis Rose and Jonathan Yardley (whose observations on Dickens come from Norrie Epstein's book), or as with reports from numerous primary publications (like Australia's *Gold Coast Bulletin* and Germany's science-news magazine *Geo*) that have found their way to me secondarily through the far-ranging monthly compendium *The Fortean Times* . . . a number of sources have been subsumed into other credited bodies.

And, alas, this lifelong taker-of-notes and clipper-of-oddments suddenly finds himself with a few very beautiful pieces of verbal flotsam that have been, over time, altogether freed from a recognizable origin. I wish I did know, for instance, from where I'd lifted Charles Baxter's incisive understanding of Captain Ahab; but I can only hope that he and a handful of others believe my willingness to credit them stood firm, even as my piles of notepad pages and cocktail napkins and make-do backs of crumpled supermarket receipts grew ever more tottery.

⌣

Anonymous Babylonian: *Gilgamesh* (N. K. Sandars translation); Ansen, David: "Out From Under the Taliban" (in *Newsweek*); Atkinson, D. T.: *Magic, Myth and Medicine;* Banville, John: *The Newton Letter;* Barnes, Edward: "Two-Faced Woman" (in *Time*); Bartusiak, Marcia: *Through a Universe Darkly;* Barzun, Jacques: *From Dawn to Decadence;* Bates, Marston: *Gluttons and Libertines;* Begley, Sharon: "The War Over Stem Cells" (in *Newsweek*); Bernier, Olivier: *The World in 1800;* Birkerts, Sven: "The Grasshopper on the Windowsill" (in *Readings*); Brauer, Jr., George C.: *The Decadent Emperors;* Brenner, Frederic: *Jews / America / A Representation;* Brown, Eric: "I Was a Teenage Space Opera!" (in *Comic Book Marketplace*); Casson, Lionel: *Travel in the Ancient World;* Cissell, Michael and Monica: conversation; Clarens, Carlos: *An Illustrated History of Horror and Science Fiction Films;* Constantine, Peter: *Japanese Street Slang;* Cortázar, Julio: *Around the Day in Eighty Worlds;* Cummings, Ray: *The Girl in the Golden Atom;* Davidson, Abraham A.: *The Eccentrics and Other American Visionary Painters;* Dickens, Charles: *David Copperfield* (and other works); DC (National Comics):

various adventures of "The Legion of Super-Heroes" and "Space Ranger"; Doyle, Arthur Conan: *Our American Adventure;* Eager, Edward: *Half Magic;* Eckstein, Gustave: *The Body Has a Head;* Edwardes, Allen: *Erotica Judaica;* Ehrenreich, Barbara: "Welcome to Cancerland" (in *Harper's Magazine*); Eisler, Robert: *Man Into Wolf;* Eliot, George: *Daniel Deronda* (and other works); Elkins, James: *Pictures of the Body* and *What Painting Is;* Epstein, Norrie: *The Friendly Dickens;* Ferris, Timothy: *Coming of Age in the Milky Way* and *The Whole Shebang;* Fiedler, Leslie: "Introduction" (to the Prometheus Books edition of *The Star Rover*); Filbert, Nathan: conversation; Finger, Stan: "Did Wichitan Lead Double Life?" (in *The Wichita Eagle*); Folger, Tim: "Quantum Shmantum" (in *Discover*); Glory, Child of, aka Smith, Les [pseudonyms]: "My Mastectomy" (in manuscript); Goldbarth, Albert: "Introduction" (for *The Measured Word,* ed. Kurt Brown); Grahame, Kenneth: *The Golden Age;* Green, Jonathon: *The Big Book of Filth;* Greenstein, Jesse: "An Introduction to 'The Dyer's Hand'"; Gribbin, John: *The Little Book of Science;* Gunn, James: *Alternate Worlds: An Illustrated History of Science Fiction;* Hahn, Kimiko: "The Shower" (in *Volatile*); Haining, Peter: *The Fantastic Pulps;* Haramundanis, Katherine: "A Personal Recollection" (see: Payne-Gaposchkin, Cecilia); Kidwell, Peggy A.: "An Historical Introduction to 'The Dyer's Hand'"; JB: "Plastic Pointers" (in *FHM*); Johnson, Paul: *The Birth of the Modern;* K., Kendall: correspondence; Klingaman, *The First Century;* Komarnicky, Linda and Rosenberg, Anne: *What to Do If You Get Breast Cancer;* Larson, Gary: "Oh my God, Bernie!" (a *Far Side* cartoon); Lawrence, D. H.: "The White Horse" (in *The Complete Poems of D. H. Lawrence*);

The Levenger Catalogue, Autumn 2000 (catalogue copy for "Platinum Celluloid Fountain Pen"); London, Jack: *The Star Rover;* Longus: *Daphnis and Chloe;* Lovelace, Skyler: conversation; Matthews, William: "The Penalty for Bigamy Is Two Wives" (in *Sleek for the Long Flight*); Melville, Herman: *Moby-Dick* (and other works); Menand, Louis: "False Fronts" (in *The New Yorker*); Moskowitz, Sam: *Under the Moons of Mars;* Otis, Laura: *Membranes: Metaphors of Invasion in Nineteenth-Century Literature, Science and Politics;* Ovid: *The Metamorphoses* (Horace Gregory translation); Palmer, William J.: *The Highwayman and Mr. Dickens;* Panek, Richard: *Seeing and Believing; Parade,* "The Sunday Newspaper Magazine": "Did actor David Duchovny use a 'butt double' . . . ?" (letter to Q&A column); Patchett, Ann: *Bel Canto;* Payne-Gaposchkin, Cecilia: *The Dyer's Hand: An Autobiography* (edited by Katherine Haramundanis); Pepys, Samuel: *The Sayings of Samuel Pepys* (edited by Richard Ollard); Pliny the Elder: *Natural History* (John F. Healy translation); Polo, Marco: *The Travels* (Ronald Latham translation); Pool, Daniel: *Dickens' Fur Coat and Charlotte's Unanswered Letters;* Rickard, Bob and Michell, John: *Unexplained Phenomena;* Rosten, Leo: *The Joys of Yiddish;* Rubin, Saul: *Offbeat Museums;* Russel, Sean: *Gatherer of Clouds;* Schmidt, Michael: *Lives of the Poets;* Sedaris, David: *Naked;* Sedgwick, John: "The Foreskin Saga" (in *GQ*); Shlain, Leonard: *Art & Physics;* Simak, Clifford D.: *Shakespeare's Planet;* Silverberg, Robert (writing as Ivar Jorgenson): *Starhaven;* Spears, Richard A.: *Slang and Euphemism;* Thackeray, William Makepeace: *Pendennis;* Thompson, C. J. S.: *Ladies or Gentlemen?;* Tyrangiel, Josh: "Did You Hear About . . ." (in *Time*); *U.S. News and World Report:* "Mysteries of History" Special

Edition; Whitman, Walt: *Specimen Days;* Wilbur, Richard: "Poetry and Happiness" (in *Shenandoah*); Yalom, Marilyn: *A History of the Breast;* Zacks, Richard: *History Laid Bare;* Zimet, Jaye: *Strange Sisters.* I am also indebted to about a jillion issues of four of the weekly supermarket tabloids: *The Globe, The National Enquirer, The National Examiner,* and *The Sun;* and, indispensably, to my years'-worth of reading (sometimes credulously, sometimes skeptically) in *The Fortean Times.* Special thanks to three of the alpha wolves: Fiona McCrae, Anne Czarniecki, Jeff Shotts. No part of this book was researched, written, or submitted for publication via computer.

∽

Pieces of Payne was completed—I suppose I should say that the *manuscript* of *Pieces of Payne* was completed—in the final days of 2001 and mailed to Graywolf Press on January 2, 2002. And yet the *elements* of *Pieces of Payne* are never completed. They go on, noticed or not, the way that the life of Henry Foker continues along the underside of the pages of Thackeray's novel *Pendennis:* unstoppably, if we attend to his doings; and equally unstoppably if we don't. The beginning of chapter 45: "The noble Henry Foker, of whom we have lost sight for a few pages, has been in the meanwhile occupied, as we might suppose a man of his constancy would be, in the pursuit and indulgence of his all-absorbing passion of love." In a way—despite the previous list of acknowledgments—*Pieces of Payne* has no sources; it simply takes its place among elements that precede it and that follow it . . . that thrive along its underside.

Of unconnected body parts, *The Fortean Times* for

March 2002 reports "an Afro-Caribbean boy aged about five, whose headless and limbless torso was found floating in the Thames. It is thought that he may have been the victim of African *sangomas* (witch doctors) who used his body parts for 'muti' medicine." From the same issue: "After an anonymous tip-off, police in Togo found ceramic pots containing a hunchback's hump, vulture eggs, hyena paws and a panther's pelt when they raided Pastor Koukouvi Agbekossi's Church for the Adoption."

Does this latter get filed under "chopped-up bodies" *or* under "human-animal mergers"? Also from March 2002: "A mother bear appears to have cared for a missing 16-month-old Iranian toddler, who was found safe and sound three days later in the animal's den, and had probably been nursed by it." Does this get clipped for filing under "human-animal mergers"? Under "oddball tales of suckling"? Under "miraculous returns"?

The National Examiner for July 16, 2002, has this fresh contribution to "miraculous returns": "Two Norwegian boys, Orjan and Robert Drag Mikalsen, 11 and 10, were fishing near Rorvik and hooked a cod with a man's golden engagement band in its mouth—lost 14 years ago by the fiancé to Orjan's cousin!" In that same issue, we learn of how actor Dan Ackroyd's wife Donna Dixon "spotted a familiar silver ring with a gold cross in a newspaper spread of items recovered from Ground Zero in the aftermath of 9/11. Donna had given the ring to actor Anthony Perkins' widow, Berry Berenson, who was aboard American Airlines Flight 11 when it crashed into the north tower. 'Donna opened up the paper and there it was.'"

And this same issue, not yet squeezed clean of its fascinations, tells us that a "Woman [from Wichita, Kansas, which has figured in this book a few times already] Gives Birth to Two Sets of Identical Twins—At the Same Time! They're 1-in-25-Million!" And of twinning worth attention, *The Wichita Eagle* for July 9, 2002 says that "Nocebo Effect is Evil Twin of Placebo Effect": "While the placebo effect refers to health benefits produced by a treatment that should have no effect, patients experiencing nocebo effect experience the opposite. They presume the worst, health-wise, and that's what they get."

These pieces won't halt: the boundary of a book is less than air to them. These pieces wink at each other, they shnoogle sighingly, they meet to confer, they part, they wave *adieu* and zip toward different mental planet zones, they reproduce, they tease us with coherence, they grimace and coil about and finagle, they repeat one another, they flaunt, they taunt, they sail away. Maybe only a deity—if deities exist—explains (or *is*) these splinters' unity. Heraclitus wrote, "God is day and night; winter, summer; war, peace; satiety, hunger—all of the opposites, this is the meaning."

For us, however—stuck in our urgent, stumble-step human limitedness—a day can be an opaque thing; and its breakthrough sparkles of light can be reformative in ways that are both glorious *and* unsettling. Of Carter Horton, the hero of Clifford D. Simak's *Shakespeare's Planet:* "He sat, waiting, and again there was a stirring in his mind, as if something had entered it and was striving to form a message there, to draw a picture there. Slowly, by painful degrees, the picture grew and built, at first a shifting, then a blur, and, finally, hardening into a cartoon-like representation that changed and changed again and yet again, becoming clearer and more definitive with each change until it seemed that there were two of him—two hims squatting there beside the Pond."

Two hims.

The book goes on; and they continue.

The book is over, it closes; and they continue.

July 16, 2002

ALBERT GOLDBARTH was born in Chicago, Illinois, and currently lives in Wichita, Kansas. He has been publishing notable collections of poetry and of essays for over a quarter of a century, from presses large and small, and is the recipient of three fellowships from the National Endowment for the Arts, a Guggenheim fellowship, and the National Book Critics Circle Award in poetry two times. His previous collections of essays are *A Sympathy of Souls, Great Topics of the World, Dark Waves and Light Matter,* and *Many Circles,* which received the PEN Center USA West award for creative nonfiction; his most recent volume of poetry is *Saving Lives.*

The text of *Pieces of Payne* has been set in Calisto,
a typeface designed by Ron Carpenter.
Book design by Wendy Holdman.
Set in type by Stanton Publication Services, Inc.
Manufactured by Friesens on acid-free paper.

Graywolf Press is a not-for-profit, independent press. The books we publish include poetry, literary fiction, essays, and cultural criticism. We are less interested in best-sellers than in talented writers who display a freshness of voice coupled with a distinct vision. We believe these are the very qualities essential to shape a vital and diverse culture.

Thankfully, many of our readers feel the same way. They have shown this through their desire to buy books by Graywolf writers; they have told us this themselves through their e-mail notes and at author events; and they have reinforced their commitment by contributing financial support, in small amounts and in large amounts, and joining the "Friends of Graywolf."

If you enjoyed this book and wish to learn more about Graywolf Press, we invite you to ask your bookseller or librarian about further Graywolf titles; or to contact us for a free catalog; or to visit our award-winning web site that features information about our forthcoming books.

We would also like to invite you to consider joining the hundreds of individuals who are already "Friends of Graywolf" by contributing to our membership program. Individual donations of any size are significant to us: they tell us that you believe that the kind of publishing we do matters. Our web site gives you many more details about the benefits you will enjoy as a "Friend of Graywolf"; but if you do not have online access, we urge you to contact us for a copy of our membership brochure.

www.graywolfpress.org

Graywolf Press
2402 University Avenue, Suite 203
Saint Paul, MN 55114
Phone: (651) 641-0077
Fax: (651) 641-0036
E-mail: wolves@graywolfpress.org